JANE DALY

# Billionaire and the Baker

## Jane Daly

# Chapter 1

Of all the dresses in her closet, why had Lauren picked this one? Oh, yeah, because she needed to do laundry. A sharp thread jabbed the back of her neck. The waistband cut into her stomach every time she breathed, and she had to pee.

She should have let her employee Kennedy help the customer now leaning over to inspect the muffins in the display case. He'd better hurry.

"May I help you?" Her brusque words didn't have the desired effect of encouraging him to make a choice. He continued to stare into the case as if waiting for something to magically appear.

Four choices, dude. Pick one.

"Do you have any bagels?"

The man straightened and Lauren noticed three things. His suit fit like a second skin. His eyes were the crisp blue of a spring day. And his accent. Why did he have to be from South Africa? That was an accent she'd tried to forget.

Lauren swallowed against the sarcastic response begging to be unleashed on his unsuspecting person. "No. Only muffins."

"I see."

Lauren fisted her apron in one hand until her nails dug into the soft flesh of her palm. "What can I get you?" Please make it snappy.

His intense blue eyes bored into hers. "Why don't you have bagels?"

Lauren inhaled through her nose and exhaled to the count of five.

"This is Muffin Top Bakery. Hence the selection of muffins." This time she couldn't help the sarcasm. This guy was getting on her last nerve. If his ridiculous question wasn't enough, that accent pushed her to the edge of civility.

"I'll take an orange bran muffin." He sighed as if her inability to produce a bagel from thin air was the unforgiveable sin.

Using tongs, Lauren retrieved his choice. "For here or to go?" She held the muffin aloft.

"For here."

Lauren placed the orange bran on a plate and set it on the counter along with a fork. "Anything else?"

"A cup of tea, please. Milk, no sugar."

She pointed to twin carafes on the coffee bar in the center of the dining area. "Coffee only. No tea." She threw him a pointed glare, one she hoped would quell further questions. It didn't work.

The guy's lip curled. Actually curled. "No tea?"

Her breathing quickened. She needed to vamoose, like now, before she blasted this guy. Or lost control of her bladder.

"Excuse me a moment." Lauren spun and strode into the back room.

Kennedy sat on a stool at the broad table they used

for mixing, baking, and filling muffin tins, face glued to her cell.

"Kennedy, can you please ring up Mr. Snooty South Africa? I have to pee."

"Huh?"

Lauren hooked a thumb toward the front room. "Please help the guy out there?"

Kennedy slid off her stool with a frown. "How do you know he's from South Africa?"

"Just go. I'll tell you later."

She used the restroom then plopped down on Kennedy's vacated stool. She shouldn't let a customer irritate her, but his accent … Memories bubbled up from a place she thought she'd locked down. Apparently not tight enough.

Kennedy returned, fanning herself with one hand. "Whew. He's smokin' hot."

Lauren grimaced. "He's annoying."

"I could put up with a lot of annoying if my guy looked like that. And the accent. Where did you say he's from? And how did you know?"

"I once knew someone from South Africa." Lauren turned toward the kitchen. "I'm going to clean up."

Lauren could feel her coworker staring a hole in her back.

"Why was he so annoying?" Kennedy hip-bumped Lauren away from the sink. "Here, let me do that." Kennedy plunged her hands into the soapy water.

"First, he wanted a bagel." Lauren leaned back against the counter. "Then he wanted tea, not coffee." She mimicked his accent. "Tea, a splash of cream, no sugar."

Kennedy sent a sly smile in Lauren's direction. "I

hope he comes back tomorrow. I'm happy to wait on Mr. South Africa."

Lauren shook her head. "I'm going to let Molly out for a potty break."

Climbing the stairs, Lauren congratulated herself for the millionth time for hiring Kennedy. Despite her shoulder-to-wrist tattoos and purple spiked hair, she was by far the best employee ever. No one would guess the forty-something woman was raising her fifteen-year-old nephew after Kennedy's sister died.

Lauren opened the door to her apartment above Muffin Top Bakery and paused to catch her breath. Those extra pounds she'd gained since opening the bakery refused to let go. She joked they would be with her into eternity, just like her relationship with God. Eternal security for chunky women.

Molly whined from her kennel the minute Lauren stepped into her apartment.

"Good girl, Molly." Lauren unhooked the kennel door. The dog bounded out and jumped up on Lauren's apron.

"No, girl. Down." She gently pushed the puppy to the floor. "Let's get your harness and go outside."

A few weeks into her service dog training and Lauren hoped she'd be deemed ready to move up to the next level. Sometimes it was hard to tell if a puppy would turn out to be an appropriate companion to a blind or deaf person.

Lauren slipped the harness over Molly's squiggling body and went to the door leading outside. Lauren wasn't ready to let the pup into the bakery. She still jumped on people.

They bounded down the steps, and Lauren released

Molly to do her business on the bushes against the fence separating her property from next door. Lauren breathed in the humid air of a New York summer. The previous owner had planted roses along the fence line and their sweet smell wafted toward her on the slight breeze. Lauren kicked off her shoes and let the grass tickle the bottoms of her feet.

Molly returned and sniffed Lauren's bare legs. "Let's go for a short walk." Before Lauren could reattach the harness, Molly dashed away and lunged at someone walking down the sidewalk.

"No!" Lauren yelped as Molly planted her paws on the thighs of Mr. Snooty South Africa.

Paul leaned forward to speak to his driver. "Drop me here, won't you? I need to stretch my legs."

"Sure thing, Mr. Montrose," replied Marvin, his driver and personal assistant.

Paul shoved the papers he'd been reviewing into a satchel and climbed out of the SUV. A walk would do him good before his first day at the bank. He patted the upper pocket of his suit coat to ensure he'd brought the packet of antacids. No telling what type of stress today would bring. He shouldn't be nervous about meeting his new employees. He'd faced many adversaries around a board room table. Today should be a piece of cake.

The village of Hornell stirred to life, reminding Paul of his hometown. Old buildings like solemn sentinels lined the downtown street. Somewhere a clock chimed the quarter hour. Paul consulted his Rolex and decided he had time to duck into the little bakery he passed. He deserved a treat after the past week's self-deprivation.

The bakery sat by itself in the middle of a row of mixed-use buildings, surrounded by a small garden. No, not a garden. A yard. He must continue to speak American, not the British English he'd spoken during his stay there.

Thinking about England brought a pang of grief for his parents. What would they say about his emigrating to America?

Ducking his head to avoid the low entrance, he strode to the display case to consider the offerings. Four varieties of muffins. What kind of bakery was this? Paul had his mouth set on a bagel with cream cheese. Not a hefty amount of the schmear, a mere dollop on each half.

"May I help you?" The woman's voice sounded flat and very American. Typical New Yorker. Impatient.

"Do you have any bagels?" He'd have thought his question, innocent as it was, wouldn't have unleashed a barrage of sarcasm. And his request for a cup of tea resulted in the same disdain.

The only redeeming thing about his spontaneous decision to duck into this particular business was the woman herself. Paul's breath caught as their eyes met. Hers were brown. Or maybe green. But the intensity with which she stared at him was at once unnerving and encouraging.

Most likely encouraging him to make a hasty exit. When she'd disappeared through a curtained doorway, Paul felt a sense of loss. She was pretty but obviously ill-tempered. Not a great combination, especially in the service industry.

The muffin exceeded his expectations. Warm, crusty on top and wonderfully chewy on the inside. He cut it in half, not daring to eat the entire thing. The calorie count in this baked good was probably over four hundred.

By the time Paul finished his muffin half, his watch indicated he should make his way to the bank for his first day. Patting his pocket, he was assured of the presence of the antacids. At least he didn't need them yet.

Carrying the disposable coffee cup outside, he pointed himself in the direction of the bank and along the white picket fence leading from the bakery to the corner of the yard.

"Good heavens!" Paul jumped when a tiny beast exploded from the yard and lunged toward him. He raised a hand to fend off the attack and instantly regretted the reaction when he felt the hot coffee splash down the front of his suit.

"Blast," he exclaimed, watching the creamy liquid slide down his jacket.

"I'm so sorry," a woman said. "She's still a puppy."

As if that was an acceptable excuse for ruining his suit. He imagined the impression he would make on his first day at the bank.

Paul's mood didn't improve when he glanced up from the disaster to see the annoying woman from the muffin shop. She wrestled the excited dog until she snapped the leash to the mutt's harness. Not soon enough.

"I'll run inside and get a towel." She seemed to reconsider. "Or some napkins."

"Fine. Quickly please. I'm in a hurry." Stupid mutt.

The brown-haired woman spun and dragged her dog into what he assumed was the back door of the bakery he'd just vacated.

She returned moments later, without the mutt, and handed him a white towel. He wiped his damp jacket, leaving white fuzz on the blue fabric.

"I'll pay for dry cleaning," the woman said.

"No." Paul bit his tongue to keep from speaking words he'd regret. This suit cost him more than two thousand dollars. He couldn't just toss it into some Podunk dry cleaner and expect it back in the same pristine condition. "I have someone who will take care of it for me."

"At least let me pay for it," she offered.

"Hardly necessary." His assistant would likely whisk away the suit and have it back at the house before Paul noticed it was gone.

Thrusting the damp towel in her direction, he stopped to assess the damage. Hopefully no one would notice the slightly darker area of his suit coat. First impressions were of vital importance.

Looking up, he noticed the woman was still staring at his jacket. "Thank you for the assistance." Actually, the whole misfortunate event was her doing. He took a step back. Anything to get away from an awkward introduction.

"Again, I apologize," the woman said. "How can I make it up to you? I mean, if you won't let me pay to have your jacket cleaned . . ."

Before he could respond, she stuck her hand out. "I'm Lauren. Lauren Jensen."

Paul hesitated, but protocol dictated he do the right thing. He sighed and grasped her hand. No sense in giving his last name. People tended to get weird when they found out who he was. "Paul."

The woman's smile lit her face. "If you come to my shop tomorrow, your muffin and coffee are on me."

"As opposed to my coffee being completely on me." He gestured toward his suit.

She looked stricken. "Again, I'm so sorry. The dog—"

"Is still a puppy." He nodded. "I got that part already."

She swallowed as if she realized how insufficient the excuse was for the damage. He nearly told her not to worry about it, then recalled her testy attitude when she waited on him earlier. Would he be back the next day? The muffin he'd consumed tasted fabulous. Too bad tea was not on the menu at this small establishment.

Paul dropped his hand to his side. Was this unfortunate accident God's reminder that he had no business eating baked goods for breakfast? Did skipping sugar in his coffee count? He'd weigh himself the minute he returned to his rented Air B&B.

The woman hadn't moved, probably waiting for his response.

Paul cleared his throat. "Thank you, but that also won't be necessary."

Before she could respond, Paul spun on his heel and walked down the sidewalk toward the bank. He pulled his cell from the inside suit pocket and told Siri to call his assistant.

"Marvin, I'm going to need you to take my suit to the cleaners when I get back."

"Certainly. Would you like me to bring a fresh jacket?"

Paul glanced down at the fuzz that seemed to point to the coffee stain. "Perhaps that would be best."

"Where shall I meet you?"

Judging the distance to the bank, Paul decided he preferred to arrive on his first day with a clean suit. Closer to the scene of the accident than to the bank, he spoke the address for The Muffin Top into the phone. "Ten fifty-one Main Street."

"Be right there." His assistant ended the call.

What would he do without Marvin? For one thing, he'd begin his day at his new bank with a ruined suit. Paul's stomach began its slow churn. How would the staff respond to him? He'd purchased the failing bank as a strategic addition to his portfolio. After months of waiting, the FDIC finally approved the sale.

He owned a bank. Dad would have been pleased.

The luxury SUV pulled to the curb and Paul climbed into the back.

"Here you go, Sir." Marvin handed him a garment bag.

Paul slipped out of the damp suit jacket and thrust his arms into the sleeves of the replacement. "Thank you, Marvin."

"I'll get this cleaned right away." Marvin took the discarded jacket and inspected the spot. "Not tea?"

"Apparently tea is not on the menu." Paul inclined his head toward The Muffin Top.

Marvin wrinkled his nose. "Coffee?"

"It was coffee before some woman—" He compared the replacement suit jacket against his pants. "How does this look?"

Marvin's white teeth were a contrast to his ebony skin as he smiled at Paul in the rearview mirror. "Not a perfect match, but close enough."

"Close enough." Paul repeated the phrase to reestablish his composure.

Marvin pulled onto the street and drove the short distance to First Upstate Bank. "I can drive you to the bank each day."

Paul considered. "My suit would have survived the trip if not for some crazy woman and an even crazier puppy."

Marvin eyed him in the mirror. "Sounds like there's more to the story."

"Just let me out here." Paul reached for the door handle. "Besides, I need the steps."

# Chapter 2

**Once Molly was** sufficiently scolded and loved on, Lauren put the pup back into the kennel and returned downstairs to the shop. Kennedy had finished cleaning the kitchen and was wiping down the counters.

"Thanks, Ken. You wouldn't believe what just happened."

Kennedy set the rag on the counter. "And you won't believe what I just saw."

"You first," Lauren said, dropping onto her favorite stool.

"You know that hot South African guy? Someone just pulled up in an Escalade and the guy got in the back seat. The back seat! Like he had a driver or something. Do you think he's rich?"

Lauren put her hand on her forehead. "Ugh. I hope . . . well, I don't know what to hope." Lauren groaned. "When I got Molly outside, she pulled the harness out of my hand and jumped up on that guy. He inadvertently spilled his coffee down his suit."

Kennedy sighed. "Sounds like a meet-cute."

"You read too many romance novels."

Kennedy shrugged. "It's the only romance I get."

"You could date."

"Ha. As if. No one wants a forty-year-old woman who's tied down to a sulky fourteen-year-old." She picked up the rag and shook it in Lauren's direction. "But you on the other hand."

"No way. I don't have time to date." Besides, no man wanted a fat girlfriend. Lauren grabbed the extra flesh she'd put on in the past two years. Maybe some of it would melt off while training Molly. All those walks had to have some impact on her weight. Right?

She slid off the stool. "I'm going to check the coffee situation."

In the dining area, Lauren greeted a couple of the regulars and made small talk while refilling the thermoses with fresh coffee. Her thoughts turned to Mr. Snooty. Paul. His hand had been warm, engulfing hers with a nice squeeze. Most guys wanted to crush her fingers, asserting their authority. Or so Lauren thought.

Should she take up his suggestion and offer tea in addition to coffee? While she bustled around, sweeping crumbs off tables and tossing discarded cups, Lauren mentally calculated the cost of adding hot teas to the menu. Would there be a return on investment and would it be enough to cover the additional cost?

The mental calculations kept her busy. Not busy enough. She couldn't get the picture of Molly's paws on Paul's suit out of her mind. It would be funny if she hadn't been so embarrassed. He'd been gracious enough, declining her offer to have his suit cleaned.

Still, despite his snootiness and his resemblance to the guy whose name she refused to utter, Lauren hoped he'd be back tomorrow. Kennedy was right. The guy was hot. Intense blue eyes like photos she'd seen of the

Alaskan glaciers. Sandy brown hair, neatly cut and combed to one side. With his strong jaw and perfect fitted suit, he'd look at home on the cover of a magazine.

Speaking of magazines, it was time to call her sister. Lauren made a mental note to call Samantha after they closed.

Kennedy poked her head through the door from the kitchen to the dining room. "I'm gonna take a break. That okay with you?"

"Sure. When you come back, I'm going to the bank."

Kennedy nodded and disappeared into the kitchen. Lauren glanced around the dining area with a satisfied smile. After two years, she'd finally turned a small profit. A few regulars came every day and one of the older ladies asked if her book club could meet there after Lauren closed at two. Lauren agreed, as long as they bought a few muffins.

The lady agreed and the arrangement was working so far. Lauren considered offering the same to the ladies' Bible Study at her church. They currently met at the library, but some of the women had complained they couldn't bring their travel mugs of coffee into the building.

Lauren made another mental note to follow up with her pastor's wife.

While Kennedy was outside, Lauren prepared the day's bank deposit.

"I'll be back shortly," Lauren told Kennedy when she'd returned from her break.

"Anything you need me to do?"

Lauren pointed to her recipe binder. "See if you can

find my recipe for pumpkin spice muffins."

Kennedy rolled her eyes. "You sure you want to jump on that bandwagon?"

"Why not? The entire country is pumpkin spicing. Why not us?"

"You got it."

Lauren shoved the bank bag into her purse and headed down the sidewalk toward the bank. Soon there'd be snow and business would slow down. After her loan payment today, she'd be able to tuck away some money to tide her over during the slower winter months.

As long as nothing bad happened.

Paul stepped through the door of the ancient brick building and inhaled. Though not as ancient as the buildings in London, the lobby had the distinctive smell common among old buildings. Worn, dusty, and homey. Fifty years ago, the furnishings may have been fashionable. Now they looked old and shabby, like a well-worn but comfortable sofa.

The New Accounts representative stood from her desk inside the door and greeted him with a smile. "Good morning. How may I help you?"

"I'm Paul Montrose."

The woman extended her hand across the desk. "It's a pleasure to finally meet you, Mr. Montrose. I'm Carol Watson."

Paul shook Carol's hand. "Please, call me Paul."

"The board is waiting for you in the conference room." She turned and pointed toward a bank of glass windows. "There's coffee and donuts."

Paul grimaced. The muffin and coffee he'd consumed churned in his stomach. He should have known better. After weeks of denying himself anything resembling a carb, his stomach did not appreciate the baked good now sitting like lead in his belly. No time to unobtrusively open the antacid packet.

He glanced around the bank lobby. The teller area had four windows and only two of them had employees sitting or standing behind the counter. From the new accounts desk, he could see the operations supervisor sitting at her desk behind the teller line. He counted a total of five employees, not including anyone in the conference room.

"Thank you, Carol," Paul said. "It's a pleasure to meet you."

"Let me know if I can get you anything."

Paul took a deep breath, held it for the time it took him to cross the lobby. He exhaled and opened the door.

The board members hailed him with handshakes and back slaps, typical of the American's exuberant greeting he was becoming used to.

"Glad you made it, Paul."

"Thank you, Chandler."

Paul recognized Chandler Daniels from the Zoom calls they'd had regarding the sale of the bank.

Chandler quickly took control of the meeting. "Let's all have a seat and get this party started."

"Before we begin," Paul said, "I want to thank Mr. Chandler Daniels. He has been instrumental in helping me wade through the Federal Deposit Insurance Corporation's myriad demands. Many times I was tempted to quit the whole thing. But Chandler's calm assurance and steady leadership helped me finish the deal. Thank you."

Paul's announcement was met with  a round of applause. It was a shame Chandler wasn't in a financial position to purchase the ailing financial institution. He'd make a fine CEO. Paul tucked that thought into his back pocket to think about in the future. When he was ready to move onto his next acquisition.

Chandler Daniels took control of the meeting. "Okay, gentlemen and Ms. Livingston, you have in front of you the most recent financial statements of our little bank."

Paul opened the neatly bound, CPA prepared financials. First Upstate Bank was splashed across the top of each page, along with the bank's logo. Paul knew from his research that changing the name of the bank would require another lengthy FDIC process. One he wasn't willing to do. At least not for the foreseeable future.

Chandler guided the rest of the board line by line through each of the pages. Paul had pored over them multiple times, so he took the opportunity to observe the three men and one woman sitting around the table. He mentally rehearsed their names. Chandler Daniels, Martha Livingston, Andrew Roth, Alex Gonzales, Mark Henderson. With the exception of Alex, who looked like he could be of Hispanic origin, all were White.

Paul shook his head. Rural New York was different from The City. He hoped his assistant, Marvin, would be treated well. Apartheid might be unlawful in South Africa, but racism still existed there. Here in the US, too, Paul had observed.

Chandler's voice broke through Paul's meanderings. "Does anyone have any questions?"

Martha adjusted her glasses on her long and somewhat pointed nose. Her silver and black hair was cut short, emphasizing her narrow face. "What changes do you plan to help get us back on track?" Her question sounded more like a challenge.

Paul smiled and spread his hands. "Great question, Martha. I do have some ideas, but in my experience, it's best to be slow to make changes right away."

Martha seemed mollified by his use of her name. Confrontation averted. For now.

"Today's meeting is for me to meet you all in person. I want an opportunity to look at the bank operation from a thirty-thousand-foot level before implementing any changes." Paul made eye contact with each one of the board. "With your approval, of course."

The atmosphere in the room relaxed as everyone seemed to exhale simultaneously. Good. His first rule of business acquisition was to make everyone comfortable. Then he could do what he did best—take a failing business and turn it into a growing concern.

"Of course," Chandler echoed. "Well, if no one has any questions, let's get some more coffee and a donut."

Chairs squeaked across the linoleum floor as the board members pushed back from the table. Paul glanced out the window facing the lobby and spied a familiar shape. Her back was turned as she stood at the teller window. But Paul could swear it was the muffin shop lady. At least she wasn't dragging that mutt with her. Not that he hated dogs. Just ones that didn't behave.

He smoothed his jacket front, remembering how she'd tried to wipe his coffee off with a towel. The muffin lady was a bank customer. His bank customer.

Paul frowned. He hoped the Muffin Top Bakery wouldn't be part of the cutting he planned for the bank.

# Chapter 3

"Hey, Carol," Lauren said, greeting the new accounts clerk as she breezed through the door of First Upstate Bank.

"Morning, Lauren. How's it going?"

"Okay, I guess." She waved the envelope holding the day's deposit. "Always a good day when I'm putting money into my account and not taking it out."

Carol grinned. "Yup."

Lauren glanced at the crowded conference room as she stepped up to the teller line.

Her favorite teller, Cheyenne greeted her with a smile. "Hi, Lauren."

Lauren hooked a thumb toward the conference room windows. "Looks like a big-wig meeting."

Cheyanne leaned forward, rested her elbows on the counter and lowered her voice. "The new owner of the bank is in there meeting with the board."

Lauren turned slightly to observe the room. "I didn't know you had a new owner."

"Oh, yeah," Cheyanne whispered. "The bank lost a bunch of money last year and some guy bought us. We're all on pins and needles wondering if we're going to be let go."

Lauren turned back to face Cheyanne. "Surely they can't fire everybody."

"We don't know. Us tellers are at the bottom of the food chain. No one tells us anything. Even Carol won't say a thing."

Lauren sent Cheyanne what she hoped was a comforting smile. "I'm sure you're fine, Cheyanne. You're a great employee. Anyway, I need to make a deposit and my loan payment."

Cheyanne became business-like. "Of course." She picked up the envelope Lauren slid across the teller window.

Lauren sneaked one more peek at the gathering of dark-suited men. One woman in the entire group. She shook her head. One woman and what, five men? A little testosterone-heavy, but typical. Although the bank had a female operations manager and a woman new accounts rep, this little financial institution was still male dominated.

But not her problem.

Cheyanne processed Lauren's deposit and began to tap in the loan number. "How many more?"

Lauren grinned. "Only two hundred sixteen more and the business will be all mine."

Cheyanne responded with a chuckle. "You can do it, girl."

"I hope so." The Small Business Loan she'd gotten to start the bakery had been a blessing. The twenty-year amortization helped keep the payments low. Living above the Muffin Top helped too.

"How's that cute puppy?" Cheyanne asked.

Lauren's mouth turned down. "She's still a work in progress. This morning, she jumped on a customer and made him dump coffee down his expensive-looking suit. He was not happy."

"Oh, no, that's so embarrassing."

Lauren sighed. "I have a lot more work to do with her before she goes back to Certified Canine Services to complete her training."

Cheyanne nodded in sympathy. "I think it's great what you're doing. Someday Molly will help someone navigate the world." She slid two receipts across the counter and tapped them with a finger.

"As long as she doesn't get into any more trouble." Lauren tucked the receipts into her purse and turned to go. She took one last look at the gathering in the conference room before waving to Carol on her way out the door.

A cloud of humid air hit her as she walked the few blocks back to her bakery, thinking about what Cheyanne had said. How does a person buy a bank? That must cost millions. As long as the new owner didn't make any major changes, Lauren would continue to make her loan payments and count the months until the business was all hers.

The warm smell of cinnamon and sugar wafted from the bakery each time the door opened. Lauren stopped to watch customers going in and coming out of the Muffin Top.

"That's mine." A smile worked its way up to her mouth.

Paul breathed a sigh of relief when the meeting ended. Chandler offered to buy him lunch, but Paul declined. The board chair's girth suggested a meal full of carbs and calories, something Paul couldn't stomach. Literally. He'd managed to chew a couple of the antacids while the board chatted.

He ran a hand down his middle, grateful the weight he'd carried most of his life was history. The battle he'd waged had been physically and emotionally exhausting. He'd have Marvin bring him some protein to carry him through the rest of the day.

"You sure you won't change your mind about lunch?" Chandler asked, pumping Paul's hand.

Paul smiled. "Thank you. But I'm going to talk with the employees."

"Good enough. I'll leave you to it, then. Call me anytime."

Chandler and the rest of the board filed out and headed for the door. Paul second-guessed his decision to stay behind. He pictured the board members gossiping about him over lunch. How many of them had Googled him and discovered his reputation. Not a bad one, but one that garnered attention from people wanting to divest him of some of his considerable wealth.

Oh well. He'd dodged that bullet. But at what cost?

As the last of the board exited the bank, Paul approached Carol's desk. Carol glanced up from her computer.

"Carol, I'm going to be in my office. I'd like to meet with each employee one-on-one."

"Of course. How can I help?"

"Before I do that, can you help me get my email set up and the log in for the bank system?"

An hour later, Paul's stomach rumbled in protest at

being empty since the muffin he'd consumed early that morning. He sent a quick text to Marvin asking him to bring him some lunchmeat and cheese.

A quick glance at his Rolex showed him the time. "Thank you, Carol. That's all for now."

"Sure thing, Mr. Montrose."

"Please call me Paul."

"Of course. Sorry." Carol clasped her hands in front her. Paul noticed her distress.

"No need to be sorry." He waited a beat. "Is everything all right, Carol?" This was the part he hated. Dealing with human resource-type issues. Much easier to swoop in, fix the problem, and leave the business not only healthier, but a part of his growing portfolio.

The woman lowered her head. When she looked up again, tears filled her eyes. "It's just that I can't afford to lose this job. My son is special needs, and my husband and I work full-time to pay for his care."

Paul leaned his hands on his desk. "I have no intention of letting you go. Or anyone for that matter." Carol didn't need to know that the changes he planned to save the bank money had nothing to do with staff reduction.

She waved a hand in front of her face. "I'm sorry, Mr.—I mean Paul. We've all been so worried."

Paul smiled with what he hoped conveyed empathy. "Of course. Please don't worry yourself."

Carol dabbed her eyes with a finger and returned to her desk. A few moments later, he tracked her progress across the lobby and behind the teller line. From his desk, he could barely see the operations manager's desk. But it was enough to know Carol was probably passing on what he'd said about staff reductions.

Marvin entered the bank carrying a paper bag and glanced around. Paul motioned for his assistant to come into the office.

"Here's your lunch, Mr. Montrose," Marvin said, placing the bag on Paul's desk with a flourish.

"Thank you, Marvin."

Marvin looked over his shoulder toward the lobby. "How's it going here?"

Paul dug into the sack and pulled out a plastic bag containing several slices of lunchmeat wrapped around hunks of cheese.

"Going well so far."

Marvin thrust a hand into his pocket and pulled out some bills. "Mind if I get change from one of your tellers?"

Paul flipped his hand. "Be my guest." He watched with amusement when Marvin approached the teller line. His assistant was a non-apologetic flirt. Since his release from prison a few years ago, Marvin flirted with any woman within breathing distance. It didn't matter if they were twenty or ninety.

"I been around men for too long, Mr. Montrose," Marvin had explained.

Flirting wasn't in Paul's DNA. It wasn't logical to lead a woman on with vague hints of romance. He preferred direct communication. Which is why he was still single at thirty-four.

Marvin was smiling as he sauntered back to Paul's office. "Nice digs, Mr. Montrose."

Paul shook his head with a smile. "Thanks."

Marvin sank onto one of the chairs facing Paul's desk. "I'll be back at five to pick you up."

"That won't be necessary. I'll walk back to the

B&B." Paul opened his portfolio and pulled out a sheet of paper. "I'd like to you to head over to the lake house and check on the contractor. Here's a punch list of things he needs to address."

Marvin glanced at the list. "You got it, Mr. Montrose." Marvin stood, folded the paper in half and tapped it on the desk. "What about dinner?"

"I'll have a salad with some of that leftover chicken."

Marvin sent him a mock salute and headed out the door.

Paul finished eating the food Marvin brought and turned his attention to the bank customers Carol had helped him gain access to. First thing would be to contact all the high-deposit and most profitable clients. He'd ask Carol to call them and make appointments. But first, he scrolled down until he found Muffin Top Bakery.

After navigating the bank's outdated software system, he found the details he wanted. Lauren Jensen DBA Muffin Top Bakery. Sole owner. Bank customer since 2022. Small Business Administration 504 loan.

Paul's stomach sank.

This was not good.

# Chapter 4

Lauren groaned when her phone alarm dinged at four thirty a.m. She dragged herself from under the soft bed cocoon and stumbled into the kitchen to start a pot of much-needed coffee.

"Good morning, Molly girl." She let Molly out of her kennel, laughing when Molly skidded across the wood floor to the front door. Grabbing a heavy sweater, Lauren followed her pup down the stairs and out into the backyard.

Light was beginning to peek on the horizon, pushing its way through a few clouds. It would be another beautiful summer day. Molly finished her business and returned to Lauren, thrusting her cold nose into Lauren's hand.

"I know, I know. It's breakfast time."

They climbed the stairs, Molly's nails clicking on the wood steps. Lauren dumped some kibble into Molly's bowl and poured herself a cup of coffee. By five o'clock she'd showered and dressed and was turning on lights in the downstairs bakery kitchen.

Kennedy had found the recipe for pumpkin spice muffins and had laid out the necessary dry ingredients before leaving the previous afternoon. Lauren soon lost herself in the routine of mixing large quantities of batter.

"Morning, Lauren." Kennedy greeted Lauren with a huge yawn.

"Oh, good. I'm glad you're here. I'm going to run upstairs and let Molly out for a bit."

"No problem. I'll start on the rest of the muffins."

Four muffin choices each day kept things simple. Once her shop grew, she'd consider adding more options. So far, no one had complained. Except Mr. Snooty South Africa. No bagels? First world problem, sir.

While Molly romped in the back yard, Lauren's thoughts returned to the snooty guy with the South African accent. He couldn't have been more different in appearance than him whose name she refused to utter. The similarity ended with the accent. She'd once thought the accent appealing. Sexy, even. But when he moved on, shredding what little self-esteem she possessed, that was the end of that.

The guy yesterday, Paul, looked rich. Everything about him screamed wealth, from his crisp white shirt down to his European leather shoes. Lauren shuddered, remembering his distaste at Molly's exuberant greeting. When he wiped down the front of his suit jacket, Lauren caught a glimpse of gold cufflinks. Seriously, who wore cufflinks in the twenty-first century?

Rich people, that's who.

Best to stop dwelling on Richie Rich. Kennedy was right, though. He was 'smoking hot.' Despite his disdain over her lack of bagels and tea.

By seven-thirty, the Muffin Top Bakery was hopping. Lauren thanked God for the great weather that brought in a steady stream of customers. Her pulse kicked up a notch when Richie Rich himself pushed through the door. She glanced into the kitchen where Kennedy was pulling out a tray of fresh muffins. No help there. Lauren would be forced to make nice.

"Good morning." She pasted on her best smile.

"Morning."

Lauren bristled at his mumbled response. "It's Paul, right?"

Paul raised his icy blue eyes to hers. "That is correct. And you are Ms. Jensen."

"What can I get you today?" She swept a hand across the display case. Sheesh, now she was Vanna White.

"Do you have any of those bran muffins like I had yesterday?"

"You're in luck. I have one left." She ducked down to the back of the bottom shelf and snagged the last orange bran muffin with a pair of over-sized tongs. "For here or to go?"

"Here, please."

"Would you like it warmed?" Lauren hoped not.

"That won't be necessary."

Lauren mentally rolled her eyes at his formal speech. Dang it. That accent was alluring. Nope, not gonna go there.

"I see you still have no tea," Paul said, cutting his eyes toward the coffee bar and back.

Lauren bit back a sarcastic response. "No, but I've considered it." Why had she said that? She'd considered it for about ten seconds before deciding adding a selection of teas wasn't worth the effort.

"I'll have a coffee, too, then." He smiled and

Lauren's breath caught. A dimple showed itself on one side of his chiseled jaw. If he was good-looking when he wasn't smiling, he was deadly when he did.

Lauren slapped a porcelain mug on the counter next to the plated muffin. "That'll be eight fifty."

Paul handed her a twenty. She made change and watched in surprise when he stuffed all the bills and coins into the tip jar.

Who was this guy? And what was he doing in rural New York State?

Paul told himself the only reason he returned to the Muffin Top Bakery was to get to know a bank customer. His usual breakfast was a hard-boiled egg or nothing. Intermittent fasting helped him from gaining back the weight he'd worked hard to shed.

"Do you have any more of those bran muffins?" Paul admired Ms. Jensen's backside as she bent over. She reminded him of a Renoir painting. Not one of the nudes, of course. More like 'Lise With A Parasol' or 'La Parisienne.' All womanly curves and warm colors.

Warmth spread from his chest to his neck, the beginnings of a flush. He raised his eyes to the decorative clock on the wall over the coffee bar before the woman caught him ogling.

He accepted the muffin and mug and headed to the coffee bar. He poured himself a cup of coffee, added a splash of milk, and carried both to an empty table. Conversations buzzed around him, the low hum of humans interacting. Paul felt a pang of loneliness. He struggled to make friends in his adopted country. Being wealthy had its advantages, but establishing relationships wasn't one of them.

Gone were the days when he could hang out with other men, taking turns buying rounds of drinks or splitting a meal. His money now insulated him from the easy give-and-take of friends working their way up corporate ladders or reaching for the next opportunity.

Paul used a wooden coffee stirrer to cut his muffin in half, then in half again. While he chewed, he observed Ms. Jensen at the register, smiling and helping customers. She wore a flowered dress with black leggings underneath. The dress flowed around her figure as she moved to pull muffins from the case.

She was polar opposite of the few women he'd escorted to various fund raisers in New York City. Those women tended to be rail-thin and allergic to anything except rabbit food. Women who never gave him a second glance when his weight topped a hundred-thirty-two kilograms now clamored for his attention. Clamored for his money was more like it.

Paul mentally slapped his forehead. He was in America now. Two hundred ninety pounds, not kilos. He guesstimated Lauren's weight at one-sixty. A bit high for her height, but she carried it well.

He'd taken the last bite of half the muffin when Marvin pushed through the door, looked around, and approached Paul's table.

"Hey, Mr. Montrose. You ready to go?"

Paul wiped his mouth with a napkin. "Almost. Let me finish my coffee."

"Mind if I grab a muffin?"

Ms. Jensen was no longer standing behind the counter. She'd been replaced by a shorter, older woman with dyed purple hair and tattooed arms.

"Sure. Need some cash?" Paul asked, reaching for his pocket.

Marvin waved him down. "I got it."

His assistant sauntered toward the counter and Paul heard him greet the cashier.

"Hello, there beautiful lady," Marvin said.

Paul pursed his lips and shook his head. Marvin had a way with women, and they seemed to adore him. If only Paul could absorb some of that charisma. He'd already annoyed the bakery's owner. How much more would she be annoyed when he started implementing some of the changes at the bank?

Paul stood and carried his plate to the rubbish bin. He tipped the uneaten half of his muffin into the pail and set the plate and his cup in a black plastic tub sitting on top of the bin.

Marvin opened the door and allowed Paul to precede him.

"Got me a pumpkin spice muffin," Marvin said. He sniffed the white paper bag with a grin. "Fresh out of the oven, too."

"Pumpkins spice, eh? Kind of early for that madness, isn't it?"

"It's never too early."

Since his incarceration, Marvin took advantage of sampling every kind of food Paul exposed him to. And never seemed to gain a pound. Lucky brute.

Paul climbed into the back of the SUV and pulled out his portfolio to review his to-do list during the short drive to the bank.

"I got your suit back from the cleaners," Marvin said, eyeing him in the rearview mirror. "No permanent damage from the coffee spill."

"Excellent. Thank you. That was fast."

"It's never surprising what a little green incentive does."

Paul shook his head with a wry smile. "Would you please find a house cleaning service for the rental?"

"Sure thing, Mr. Montrose."

Paul thanked God every day for bringing Marvin into his life. Who would have thought a felon would make an excellent personal assistant? Marvin had spent five years locked up for tax evasion and mail fraud. Paul had run into him, literally, while negotiating the one-way streets in New York. Paul had taken Marvin to the hospital and sat with him while he recuperated. When Marvin was released, Paul had been horrified to learn Marvin was homeless.

Marvin's wife divorced him, and his adult children wanted nothing to do with their father. Paul discovered Marvin had an IQ of over one-fifty and could do just about anything he put his mind to. Paul trusted Marvin to oversee his many real estate holdings and after two years, Marvin had done nothing to breach that trust.

"What's on your agenda for today?" Paul asked.

"Same old, same old," Marvin said with a grin. "I need to call the property manager at Four Fifty and get his estimate for replacing the water pump."

Paul and Marvin rarely used the names of his various investments. Instead they used the addresses. Four Fifty was one of the high-rises in New York City. Paul's holdings stretched across the country from the Atlantic to Colorado. God had gifted him with the ability to make money, and Paul gave generously to the many charities he supported.

"Let me know what he says," Paul said. "No, never mind. Just take care of it."

"Sure thing, Mr. Montrose. I'll check on the other places as well."

"How is the remodel coming?" Paul looked forward to the day he no longer had to live in the rented Air B&B in Hornell. Although the commute to Keuka Lake would be longer, he'd be able to spread out in his own place.

"I'll write up a report and have it for you when you get done today."

"Perfect." Marvin braked to a stop in front of First Upstate Bank and Paul climbed out. He leaned down to address Marvin through the open door. "While I'm thinking about it, see if the owner of the Air B&B wants to sell."

Marvin sent him a mock salute and a grin.

Carol was already at her desk when Paul unlocked the bank door and pulled it closed behind him.

"Good morning, Carol."

Carol returned his greeting while Paul retreated into his office. He booted up his computer and checked for new emails. Nothing urgent called to his attention, so he headed into the lobby to finish his one-on-one meetings with each employee.

Carol stopped him before he reached the teller line. "Paul, I made some appointments for you like you asked. I put them on your calendar. I hope that's okay."

Paul smiled at the woman's anxious expression. "Thank you, Carol. I appreciate it." She seemed to relax at his smile. He made a mental note to find out Carol's salary and see if it needed to be adjusted. Probably should do the same for every employee. Any salary adjustments would have to wait, however. First to bolster the bank's assets and do some house cleaning.

35

# Chapter 5

**Paperwork. The bane** of every business owner's existence. How difficult considering the sunshine and mild weather called her to be out of the house.

"I guess we'll work outside," Lauren told Molly, who agreed with a sharp bark and vigorous tail-wagging. "Oh, Molly, I'm going to miss you when you go back to Certified Canine Services." Six months to foster the puppy and see if her temperament would allow her to continue training.

The sun warmed her back as Lauren spread her bills other accumulated papers on the small patio table. Molly seemed impervious to the heat. Lauren laughed when Molly tried to catch a white butterfly as it flitted from the red roses to the pink ones.

The early summer heat had produced a riot of blooms. Their sweet fragrance wafted toward her in the heavy afternoon air.

Tapping her mechanical pencil against her lip, Lauren let her eyes travel around her yard. Could she live anywhere but here? She was Hornell, New York born and bred. Sure, that guy whose name she refused to utter asked her to go to New York City with him. But the traffic and constant noise drove her back to Hornell, physically and emotionally exhausted.

Too bad the pool of eligible males was over-fished. All her friends from school were either married with babies of their own or had moved to Rochester, Buffalo, or The City to pursue exciting careers. Her buddy, Mike, was the only single guy she knew.

The sun was dipping behind the low hills when she closed her laptop and piled the papers into a neat stack.

"Let's go rustle up some dinner," she said to Molly. "I'm starved and I'll bet you are too."

"I'll work the register," Lauren said when Kennedy arrived the next morning.

"You should take a break. Maybe hire someone to help out front?"

Lauren shed her apron with a wry smile. "Not yet, Ken. Maybe next year, after we see how this winter goes."

"Let me know when you want me take over." Kennedy an apron over her head and tied it behind her. "Oh, and if Mr. South Africa's guy comes in, please let me help him."

Lauren raised her eyebrows. "You mean the Black guy?"

Kennedy's blush rose from her neck to her hairline. "He's nice."

"Whatever you say, girlfriend." Kennedy usually avoided men like leprosy after her divorce. Now that she was raising her nephew, any idea of dating went down the drain.

Lauren turned the Open sign around and took a last look around the shop before customers trickled in. She sucked in a breath and exhaled on a prayer, thanking God He'd guided her to go out on a limb and start this little business. She'd been tempted to close last winter, but since then she'd taken on a couple of catering jobs for local businesses. Between that and her regulars, she was able to take a small salary and pay Kennedy a little something.

Her business plan included breaking into the wedding business. Brides were choosing cupcakes for their weddings, letting guests have a cupcake and having a smaller wedding cake. Baking cupcakes wasn't too different than muffins. She and Kennedy had experimented with some gluten free options as well.

During a break in the stream of early morning customers, Lauren did a quick inventory of the display case.

"Ken, can you bring out some more pumpkin spice?"

"Sure thing," Kennedy called from the kitchen.

Lauren glanced up when the bell over the door chimed. Her heart did a quick upbeat when Paul stepped in, ducking his head. He ran a hand over his brown hair and strode to the counter.

"Good morning, Paul." Why was her heart beating like a bongo drum?

"Hello, Ms. Jensen." He stooped to inspect the muffin choices. "My assistant recommended the pumpkin spice, but I fail to see the attraction."

Lauren forced her expression to remain neutral. "It is a popular choice."

Paul exhaled with a grimace. "I guess I'll try one."

"Coffee too?"

"Yes, please."

"Why do I get the feeling you aren't pleased with your choices?"

"I beg your pardon?"

Lauren spoke quickly to cover her embarrassment. "Coffee instead of tea. Pumpkin spice muffin instead of a bagel. It sounds like you're here under duress."

Thank goodness his eyes twinkled with amusement instead of anger.

"I apologize. I have a lot on my mind today. Perhaps that explains my abruptness."

"Perhaps."

While she rang up his purchase, Lauren's eyes took in his double-breasted suit jacket and predicable white shirt. His tie was understated, but exuded money. What was this rich guy doing in small-town Hornell, New York. His uniform seemed better suited for The City and some concrete and steel high-rise.

Lauren gave him change for the twenty he offered and again shoved the coins and bills into the tip jar.

His eyes met hers. "Perhaps I can make it up to you."

Whatever he planned to say next was interrupted by Kennedy bringing a tray of warm muffins and setting them into the case.

"No assistant today?" Kennedy asked, attempting to look innocent.

"Not today." Paul looked from Kennedy to Lauren and back. "Shall I tell him you asked about him?"

Kennedy's face diffused with color. "Oh, no. Don't bother."

Lauren stifled a chuckle as Kennedy scampered

through the door to the kitchen.

A group of three women entered the shop, chattering and laughing. Paul took his muffin and coffee cup to a table. She barely had time to think as a steady stream of customers flowed in and out of the Muffin Top.

By the time she was able to turn her attention to Paul, he'd gone. Darn. What had he planned to ask?

She returned to the kitchen and found Kennedy up to her elbows in suds. "I'll listen for the door if you want to check on Molly."

"That would be great. Thanks." Lauren dashed up the stairs and into her apartment. Molly yipped when she caught sight of her.

"Sorry, girl. Let's get you out of here." Lauren and Molly clattered down the outside staircase and into the yard. Molly raced around, chasing a butterfly and sniffing all the bushes growing along the fence.

Molly hadn't yet shed all her puppy fuzz. Lauren loved curling up on the sofa with her in the evenings. Even if she didn't make it as a service dog, Molly would make a great family pet.

"Tell you what, girl," Lauren said. "Let's go back to your kennel and I'll take you to the bank when I take my deposit."

Molly seemed in agreement and proceeded Lauren up the stairs.

"Ken, I'm gonna make up my deposit now," Lauren said, poking her head through the door from the kitchen leading into the dining area.

"That's fine. But I have to tell you something." Kennedy huffed into the kitchen, hands on her hips.

"What is it?" Lauren asked. "Was someone rude to

you?"

"No. But know that hot South African guy?"

"His name is Paul. Go on." What now?

"Well, he cut his muffin in half and threw the rest away."

"How do you know this?"

"When I came out to refill the coffee when you were helping those ladies, I saw him."

Lauren pressed her lips together to keep from grinning. Kennedy was serious about waste.

"I asked him if wanted a to go box and he said, 'that won't be necessary.' Sheez. Who does that?"

Lauren inhaled through her nose. "Maybe he didn't like it?"

"No," Kennedy exploded. "I asked him, and he said it was 'acceptable.'"

Lauren shrugged. "I don't know what to tell you. I agree it's too bad half of it went into the garbage. But he did pay for it."

Kennedy huffed out a breath. "I guess. But it irks me."

Lauren patted her employee on the shoulder. "Don't let it ruin your day, okay?"

"Fine. But if he comes back tomorrow and does the same thing ..."

"Whatever. I'm going to do my deposit and get some change."

Paul took note of the glare the clerk sent him when he dumped half his muffin into the rubbish bin. There was no need for him to explain he couldn't bring himself to eat the entire thing. The subtle hint of cinnamon and cloves, along with the moistness of the pumpkin stirred his taste buds. The pleasure center in his brain screamed for more, but the logical side reminded him of the six stones he'd taken off. No way would he go back to that weight.

After several minutes of self-flagellation, he gathered his dignity around him and left the bakery. What had possessed him to flirt with Ms. Jensen? He'd spoken without thinking the thing through. His voice mocked him. 'Perhaps I can make it up to you.' Uttering a groan, he climbed into the waiting vehicle.

"Ready, Mr. Montrose?" Marvin asked.

"Yes. Thank you." Get me to the bank where I can deal in absolutes. Numbers, spreadsheets, and projections. Not pretty women with voluptuous curves.

Paul sat in silence during the short drive to the bank. Today he'd delve more deeply into the bank's financials. His meetings with the individual staff had gone well. He'd assured them his plans did not include letting anyone go. So far, so good.

"Marvin, after you drop me off, would you please return to the muffin shop and order a dozen muffins for tomorrow?"

"Any particular kind, or an assortment?"

Paul thought for a moment, remembering the taste of the pumpkin spice. "How about six of those pumpkin ones and six assorted."

Marvin grinned. "Got ya hooked, don't it?"

Paul didn't answer.

Marvin pulled the vehicle to a stop at the curb and Paul climbed out. He stooped to address Marvin through the open door. "Here's some cash for the muffins." He pulled a hundred-dollar bill from his wallet and tossed it over the seat.

"Thanks, Mr. Montrose." Marvin reached for the cash and tucked it into his shirt pocket.

Paul straightened and turned to cross the sidewalk.

"Oof." He ran smack dab into a woman. He reached out to steady her and saw it was Ms. Jensen with that small furry beast who immediately planted paws on his trouser legs.

"I'm so sorry," she said breathlessly.

"It was my fault," Paul said, dropping his arms to his side.

"No, I wasn't paying attention. Molly had something in her mouth, and I was trying to get it from her."

"I should have paid more attention."

Paul's pulse sped up when Lauren smiled.

"We can stand here all day and argue about whose fault it is. Or we can both go into the bank."

Paul opened the door and motioned her through. "After you."

"Thanks."

He checked out her backside as she proceeded him through the door. When she whirled around, he quickly raised his eyes to hers.

"Are you a customer here too?" Lauren asked.

Paul cleared his throat. "Uh, not yet."

"It's a great bank. Friendly. And they gave me a loan for my business."

Sweat broke out under Paul's arms. He'd always been able to insulate himself from the personal side of business. But this would be different. Customers—real people—would be affected by some of the changes he had planned.

"That's wonderful," Paul muttered.

"Well, I need to make my deposit," Lauren said, tugging on her dog's harness.

Paul said hello to Carol and retreated to his office. He sank onto the ancient leather chair and rested his head in his hands.

# Chapter 6

**Lauren let Cheyanne** walk around the teller counter and bend down to pet Molly. Her pup gave the teller wet kisses. Her little tail beat against Lauren's legs like a metronome.

"She's a cutie," Cheyanne said.

"Yeah, it's gonna be hard to give her up."

"How much longer will you have her?"

Lauren slid her deposit and change request across the counter when Cheyanne returned to her side of the teller line. "About three more months."

"Aww," Cheyanne said. "That's gotta be hard."

Lauren nodded her agreement. While Cheyanne processed her deposit, Lauren shot a quick glance to the new accounts desk to see if Paul was opening an account. He wasn't there nor did she see him anywhere in the bank. She mentally shrugged. Maybe he changed his mind about opening an account.

There was something elusive about the man. Why was he here in Hornell? In a town with a population of just over eight thousand, a guy wearing a designer suit and what she assumed was an expensive watch stood out. Perhaps he was part of the Downtown Revitalization Initiative. Probably some big wig from

The City to help the poor little folks of Hornell spend their ten-million-dollar grant. He'd be gone soon and there would be no ripples from his departure.

Lauren took her change and stuffed it into her dress pocket "Thanks, Cheyanne. See you tomorrow."

The rest of the day passed in a blur. At six o'clock, Lauren changed into workout clothes and headed to the YMCA. Time to work off some calories. Or attempt to.

She dropped Molly off at Kennedy's for some attention from her and William.

"Thanks for watching Molly for me." Lauren released Molly's leash. The pup lunged for Kennedy's fourteen-year-old nephew, William.

William dropped to the floor and wrestled with Molly. Kennedy spoke in a low tone. "It's the only thing that snaps him out of his surliness. I'd love to get him a dog, but I'm just not sure he's ready for that kind of responsibility."

"Time will tell. Until then, I really appreciate your help with her. I hate to leave her locked up for a long time, even though I've been assured it's okay."

They said goodbye, and Lauren headed for the YMCA.

Her workout clothes consisted of a pair of cut off sweatpants she'd had since college and an oversized tee shirt, faded from a hundred washings. She nodded to the girl at the gym counter and scanned her ID before heading into the workout room.

After a ten-minute warmup, she stopped the elliptical machine and stepped off. Turning, she bumped into a guy stepping onto the machine next to hers.

His warm hand clasped her upper arm. "We've got

to stop meeting like this." Paul stared down at her with that devastating smile.

Nerves skittered up Lauren's back at the sound of his accent. "Is that a pickup line?" Lauren asked. What were the chances she'd run into the guy again? In a town as small as Hornell, the chances were good.

Paul threw back his head and laughed. It was an awesome sight. His normally taut features softened and his whole body relaxed. Lauren felt something stir inside. Uh oh. She'd tried to brace herself against that darn accent, but her resolve had softened when he'd smiled yesterday. And now this.

*Girl, you are in trouble.*

Paul ran a hand down the front of his t-shirt. "I can assure you that it is not a pickup line."

"Good to know." Lauren pressed her lips together. Of course, the guy wasn't trying to hit on her. Why would he? But back in the bakery …

Paul's features returned to his normal poker face. "I don't come to the gym to hit on women."

Lauren yanked on the bottom of her tee to ensure it covered the roll around her middle. "Again, good to know."

Paul ran a hand over his hair and across his chin. "However, perhaps you would let me buy you a bottled water." He crossed and uncrossed his arms. "When you complete your workout, of course."

Lauren eyed him up and down. His Under Armour workout clothes fit him like they'd been custom-made. Why would a man that good-looking notice her? Especially when she wore something that looked like she'd swung by the local Goodwill Store before hitting the gym.

She surprised herself when she said, "I guess that would be okay."

Paul cleared his throat. "Great. Fantastic. I'll meet you at the front desk in say, thirty minutes?"

"Hm. Thirty minutes." Not enough time to run home and change. But enough time to dash to the restroom, fix her hair, and swipe on some lip gloss. As if that would distract him from her size.

"Later? Earlier?"

"No, that's fine. Thirty minutes it is."

She turned and ran upstairs to the weight machines, resisting the urge to see if he was watching. She hoped not. Her butt looked huge in these shorts.

What was he thinking? Paul mentally slapped himself as he pedaled the elliptical machine. What a plonker. Lauren would think he was trying to hit on her.

*Well, aren't you?*

Yes, he was. Sort of. He'd admired her curves, her smile, and her general cheeriness. Something he lacked. Perhaps she'd be willing to go on a proper outing in the future.

He finished his workout, checked his statistics on his cell, and stepped off the machine. A quick dash to the restroom to splash his face, and he was ready to make a fool of himself at the soda machine.

Lauren was already there, gazing into the case at the selections available. She straightened as he approached.

"What can I get you?" Paul asked. Lauren's face was flushed from her workout and a sheen of sweat glistened on her forehead.

"Water. I can't drink soda, diet or otherwise, this late in the evening. The caffeine, you know."

"Of course." Paul's day usually ended around midnight. He slid his debit card into the machine and purchased two waters. They plunked down and he retrieved them, placing the first one into Lauren's waiting hand. "You must have to get up early to start baking," Paul said.

Lauren nodded as she unscrewed the cap. "Four-thirty."

Paul's eyebrows rose. "Every day?"

"Every day but Sunday and Monday. That's when I sleep in." She grinned up at him. "And go to church."

Paul considered this for a moment. He hadn't attended church regularly in forever. Maybe it was time to do so. "What church to you go to?"

"First Baptist in Danville." Lauren moved toward a couple of chairs off to the side of the lobby. "Mind if I sit? My dogs are barking."

"Dogs?"

Lauren laughed, and Paul took in the way she tilted her head to the side as her laughter filled the area. She sank onto one of the chairs and lifted her feet. "It's an expression. My feet are killing me."

She sent him a sideways glance as he sat next to her. "How long have you been in the States?"

"Not long enough, apparently." Paul took a swig of his water. "I was born in Durban and my parents moved to England when I was fifteen. After their deaths, I moved to New York. I've been here two years."

Lauren nodded and Paul noticed the gold flecks in her eyes. Those eyes were filled with sympathy.

"I'm sorry about your parents."

"It's been a few years." Paul steered the conversation away from the aching loss. He'd rather have his mum and dad back than the money they'd left him. "What time is your church service?"

Lauren's mouth dropped open, then closed. "Uh, I go to the eleven o'clock service."

"Would you mind if I attended this week?"

"Everyone is welcome at church."

Paul sucked in a breath and released it slowly. He hesitated putting himself out there after many rejections from the female sex. But this woman intrigued him in an unfamiliar way.

"Maybe I could take you to lunch after the service? If you aren't too busy, that is." Paul felt his face grow warm under Lauren's unblinking stare. When she didn't answer, he said, "Never mind—"

"No, that sounds nice," Lauren said, lowering her lashes.

Paul slapped his hands on his thighs. "Great. I'll have my assistant make reservations. Is there a place you prefer?"

"Your assistant? Is that the guy who comes into the shop sometimes and flirts with Kennedy?"

"Yes, that would be Marvin. My assistant and my driver."

Lauren's brow wrinkled. "What exactly do you do?"

"I invest in real estate. And in businesses." He hoped the simplicity of his answer would satisfy her.

"Maybe I should—"

"Do you know Chandler Daniels?"

Lauren huffed out a laugh. "Everyone knows Chandler. Why?"

"I can assure you, he can vouch for me." Paul leaned toward her and lowered his voice. "He'll tell you I'm not a serial killer or anything." He smiled, hoping his attempt at levity would help.

She continued to regard him, studying his face as if to discern his truthfulness.

"Okay," she finally said. "But how do you know Chandler?"

"How about I tell you over lunch Sunday?"

Lauren stood. "All right. But I'm going to hold you to that. I better get home and get some shut eye before my very early morning."

"I'll walk you out." Paul held the door open. When they reached her car, he waited until she was buckled in and had started the engine. He gave her a cheery wave as she drove off.

Marvin must have been watching for him, as he pulled the Escalade next to him.

"Who was that, Mr. Montrose?" Marvin asked with a grin. "Wait, isn't that the muffin lady?"

"The muffin lady's name is Lauren Jensen. And yes. I ran into her in the Y."

Paul caught Marvin's eye in the rearview mirror. "Stop grinning at me, Marvin."

"You like her," Marvin said.

"Don't make me fire you," Paul said with mock severity.

"Did you ask her out?"

Paul sighed loud enough for Marvin to hear.

"You did, didn't you? Did she say yes?"

Paul had picked up his portfolio from the seat next to him. He gave up any pretense of looking at it and tossed it onto the seat. "Yes. She said yes."

"Way to go, Mr. Montrose." Marvin's grin was as bright as the stars beginning to show in the evening sky. "Where ya gonna take her?"

"That's why I have you, Marvin. Make yourself useful and find someplace suitable for a first date."

"When?"

"Sunday afternoon. I'll be going to church in Danville at eleven. Anytime after twelve."

Marvin braked to a stop and turned in his seat. "You're going to church?"

Paul waved a finger. "Turn around and drive."

Marvin chuckled all the back to the Air B&B they'd rented. Paul shook his head in amusement.

Yeah, he was going to church. And on a date. His stomach tightened. A date. With a pretty woman. He blew out a breath. He'd set something in motion that could easily end in disaster when Lauren learned what he planned for all the SBA loans at the bank.

# Chapter 7

**Lauren barely had** time to second-guess her agreement to have lunch with Paul. Because he knew Chandler Daniels didn't make him less a stranger. Something about him reminded her of that other guy. More than the accent, it was the way he carried himself. But there the similarity ended. While Paul exuded reserve and formality, her ex was all familiarity and charm. Until his charm wore off and he showed himself to be a jerk.

At first, he'd seemed the perfect boyfriend, treating her to dinner and buying flowers. Quick with a compliment and a warm hug after an exhausting day. Until …

Lauren's phone buzzed with a text from her sister as she walked through the front door of her apartment. Molly headed to her water bowl and slurped noisily.

**Samantha**: Can you talk?

Lauren tapped her sister's photo in her 'favorites' and waiting for Sam to pick up.

"Hey, sis," Sam said. "I hope this isn't too late to call."

"I just walked in from the Y. What's up?"

Sam's voice sounded terse. "I hate to bother you,

but could you pray about something?"

"Of course." Lauren's breath hitched. She and Sam were as close as two siblings could be. Her sister was the only one she could talk to about her rocky relationship with their mom.

Samantha sighed into the phone. "I just finished a photo shoot for Dior."

Lauren felt a pang of jealousy and quickly squashed it. Samantha and she were polar opposite in size, weight, and looks. As a fashion model, Sam sported a BMI of less than eighteen and barely tipped the scale at a hundred nineteen. Her natural blond hair and blue eyes made her perfect for the runway and magazine spreads.

"Dior? That's awesome." Lauren hoped her enthusiasm didn't sound forced.

"It was. The shoot in Central Park attracted a lot of attention. Some of it unwanted."

Lauren felt a flash of alarm. "What do you mean?"

"It seems I've attracted a stalker."

"What? Did you call the police?"

"They said they can't do anything until he gets violent."

"That's ridiculous."

"I know, right? So far, he's only sent me some creepy letters."

"How did he get your address?"

"He sent them to my agent's address, care of the agency."

"What are you going to do?" A surge of adrenaline kicked in, making Lauren's fingers tingle as she gripped the phone.

"I'm not sure. I have to fly to Florida for a beach

shoot, then I'll be back in The City."

"Can't you lay low for a while?"

"I have these darn contracts I've signed. My agent won't let me breach them. She said it'll kill my career."

"Better your career than you!" Lauren paced around the small living room, followed by a whining Molly.

"Is that Molly I hear in the background?"

"I think she senses my mood. I'm worried about you, Sam."

"I'll be fine. I'll make sure I'm never alone. But please pray the stalker loses interest. Now, tell me what's new with you? How's my favorite muffin lady?"

Lauren plopped onto her blue and white striped sofa. Molly laid her head on Lauren's knee. Lauren stroked the pup's head, trying to figure out how to tell her sister about Paul.

"I met this man."

Lauren pulled the phone away from her ear at her sister's squeal. "Spill, sis."

"He's from South Africa." She held her breath, waiting for her sister's response. She didn't have to wait long.

"Uh oh. You know what happened the last time you fell in love with a guy from there."

Lauren tucked her legs up and to one side. "I know. But this is different. And who said anything about love?"

Sam sounded skeptical. "How is this different?"

"It's hard to explain. He seems older than you-know-who. I'm guessing mid-thirties. He seems mature, anyway." Lauren pictured Paul in his perfectly cut expensive looking suit. And his formal way of talking.

"What does he do?" Sam asked. "He does have a job, right?"

"He said he's in real estate. Investing in real estate. But he sounded a little evasive."

Sam's voice took on a stern tone. "You need to be careful, Lauren. For all you know, this guy could be a perv."

"He said he knows Chandler Daniels," Lauren said.

"Ha. Everyone knows Chandler Daniels. You're not going out with him, are you?"

Lauren blew out a breath. "Well, yes, I am. He asked where I went to church and then invited me to lunch after."

"Sounds innocuous. Give me his name, and I'll Google him."

Lauren wracked her brain for any indication Paul had mentioned his last name. "Uh, his name is Paul. I don't know his last name."

"Sounds like a Carrie Underwood song. 'I don't even know his last name.'" Sam inhaled. "Just be careful. I worry about you."

"I worry about you, too. You let me know if your stalker tries to contact you again, okay?" Lauren didn't know what she'd do if anything happened to Samantha.

"I will. By the way, have you talked to David lately?"

"Nope." Lauren avoided their brother and his seemingly perfect little family. It was another bullet in the ammunition their mother launched in Lauren's direction. Mom compared her to David and his wife. 'Why can't you settle down like your brother.' Or 'if you'd lose weight like your sister, you might attract a man.'

"Mom will probably delight in telling you Jeanie is pregnant again."

"Ugh. Thanks for letting me know. I'll be sure to sound suitably enthusiastic when she calls."

"Don't let her get to you, hon," Sam said. "You have your life and David and Jeanie have theirs."

Yeah, but Lauren's life consisted of trying to keep her business going, paying bills, and helping foster a potential service animal. David and his wife and their two—soon to be three—kids lived in Buffalo and were the pride of her parents' lives. And mom regularly gushed about Sam's exciting career as a fashion model in New York City. Poor little fat Lauren. Would she ever find a man?

"I should let you go," Sam said. "Text me the minute you get home from your date."

Lauren disconnected after promising to give her sister all the details. But first, she needed to obsess over what to wear to church Sunday. Something that would make her look skinny.

Or she could just not eat for the next three days.

Paul found he liked working from the previous manager's office at the bank. He was far enough from the lobby traffic while still able to observe the customers coming and going. The energy in the building when customers came and went gave him a thrill. He loved the sight and sound of money changing hands, business being done.

He'd sent Marvin back to New York City to take care of some business. Paul missed the man's constant presence. He'd become Paul's closest friend. Marvin had grinned at him like a fool when Paul asked him to make arrangements for lunch on Sunday with Lauren.

"I'm on it, Mr. Montrose," Marvin had said when Paul pressed him for details.

Paul knew from experience Marvin would not disappoint. He had three days to obsess over what Marvin planned. Until then, he'd focus on his current project—ensuring First Upstate Bank had a healthier loan to deposit ratio.

Halfway through the morning, Carol interrupted his concentration with a tentative knock.

"Paul, Mr. Druban is here making a deposit. Do you want me to send him to your office?"

Paul rubbed a hand over his head. "Remind me again who he is?"

"He's one of the top twenty-five depositors you wanted to meet."

Paul shook his head to clear it of the numbers he'd focused on. "Oh, yes, please. If he has time."

Carol stepped across the lobby and approached an older man standing at the teller line. She touched his arm and spoke, pointing toward Paul's office. Paul stood and waited for the man to finish his transaction and make his way toward Paul.

"Nice to meet you, sir," Paul said, shaking the man's hand.

"John Druban," he said, settling himself on one of the chairs facing Paul's desk. "I heard there was a new sheriff in town."

Paul searched his memory for a hint of what the man meant by 'sheriff.' Coming up empty, he merely smiled.

"Chandler Daniels said you might make some changes to our little bank."

Paul's smile faded. "I'm still working through some things before I do anything."

"Good idea. Slow pretty much describes Hornell. Not a lot of development in the past few years. Covid caused a lot of small business to go belly-up. That government grant will help the local economy and hopefully the bank can assist with financing some new start-ups."

Paul grimaced inwardly. New business start-ups were a financial risk. Most small businesses close within five years, resulting in a loss for a bank. He made a noncommittal 'hm' without replying.

"Do you golf, Paul?"

"I've been known to hack a few balls now and then."

John leaned forward. "While the weather's still nice, how 'bout I put together a foursome? We can talk about your plans for the bank and enjoy some fresh air and sunshine. How does that sound?"

"Sounds great." Except he wasn't quite ready to share his plans yet. But an invitation to golf? Yes.

"I'll make a tee time for next week. Is there any day that's better for you?"

"Probably best to not schedule for Monday or Friday. Those tend to be the busiest bank days. I like to be available in case the operations manager needs a backup."

John stood. "Of course. I'll call you when I have something set up."

They exchanged contact information and John left, stopping to have a quick chat with Carol on his way out.

Paul breathed a satisfied sigh. He'd thought his stay in Hornell would be boring. Now he had a date with Ms. Jensen and an invitation to golf with other men. Maybe this wouldn't be so bad.

# Chapter 8

**By Saturday afternoon**, Lauren was ready to drop. Business had picked up at the Muffin Top for no reason she and Kennedy could determine. Not that she was ungrateful, but the bed called her name. Loud.

But first, Molly needed to be let out and given some play time. While she wrestled with Molly over her rope toy, Lauren mentally went through her closet for something to wear for lunch with Paul the next day. It wasn't a date. Not really. Just lunch. After church.

"Keep telling yourself that," she said aloud. Molly yipped her agreement.

The last time she'd gone out was when her sister dragged her on a double date with one of her male model friends. He'd been nice enough but his disdain for her dinner choice was obvious. There was nothing Lauren liked better than a restaurant burger and fries. She'd snickered over his choice of a salad, no dressing, and absolutely no croutons.

Until her mother's voice echoed in her head. *You'll never attract a man carrying that extra weight, Lauren. Why can't you be more like your sister?*

Lauren was at the point of giving up. She'd tried all the expensive weight loss diets. But when one owned a bakery, staying thin was beyond impossible. Besides loving to bake, Lauren loved to eat. While she wouldn't be called obese, she tipped the scale at a higher BMI than the average woman.

No wonder men didn't spare her a second glance. Mom's voice whispered in her ear. *No man wants a fat girl.*

Paul hadn't seemed to be disgusted by her fleshy thighs, visible under the cut-off sweats she'd worn to the gym. Lauren shuddered. After this one lunch—not a date—he'd probably move on to someone a lot skinnier and prettier. And why not? He seemed to have the whole package. Dangerous good looks, a physique most men would kill for, and money. Or so it seemed. Maybe it was all a façade. He could be one of those men who her Texas grandpa would describe as, 'All hat and no cattle.'

What did it matter, anyway? If Paul was intent on pursuing her, he must have an ulterior motive. Like what's-his-name.

Lauren patted Molly's head, running her fingers through the soft fur between her ears. "You still have your baby fur, sweet girl." Molly licked Lauren's fingers.

"Let's go try to get some sleep, shall we?" Lauren said as they climbed the stairs to the apartment. She had no doubt Molly would fall asleep quickly, while she would lie awake worrying about tomorrow.

Sunday dawned bright and sunny. Lauren carried her mug of coffee down the stairs and let Molly out in the yard. She wrapped her robe more tightly around her waist, staving off the slight chill. It wouldn't be too many more weeks before the colors began to change, and the weather get cold. How would the snow affect her business this winter?

Last winter had been mild and business remained fairly steady. Who knew what this year would bring? Any unexpected expenses or weather issues might push her into the red financially.

She finished her coffee and returned upstairs to get ready for church. The big question today was what to wear? No jeans. They fit too snug around her waist and rear end. After flipping through her clothing choices, Lauren finally decided on a maxi skirt in navy and a flowered top with half sleeves. A solid navy sweater completed the look.

She turned to the side to examine herself in the full-length mirror on the back of the bathroom door. Ugh. Why was it so easy to put weight on and so difficult to take it off?

On that thought, she gathered up Molly and led her out to her aging Honda. "Let's get you to Kennedy's house," she told the pup.

"You look fantastic," Kennedy said, grabbing Lauren in a hug.

Lauren felt herself blush. "Thanks, but I feel fat."

Kennedy shook her head. "Girl, you've got curves. Not fat. Stop measuring yourself by someone else's ruler."

Kennedy had heard all about Lauren's fractured relationship with her mother.

"Thanks for watching Molly for me."

"Are you kidding?" Kennedy said, stooping down to fondle Molly's ears. "Molly is the only thing that can coax William out of his room." She straightened. "Any idea where you're going to lunch?"

Lauren shook her head. "Nope. No idea." Nerves skittered up her spine as she considered the upcoming lunch.

"I'm sure it'll be fun. You deserve a break."

"Yeah, yeah. I work too hard. Isn't that what you always tell me?"

Kennedy laughed. "Yup. So, I don't need to repeat it?"

"Not today."

Kennedy shooed Lauren out her door. "Bye. Don't worry about Molly."

It wasn't Molly she was worried about. It was having a conversation with a man she didn't know.

Martin dropped Paul at First Baptist Church in Dansville at five minutes before eleven. Cars filled the parking lot, and parents herded their offspring toward the open double doors.

Marvin laid his arm across the passenger seat and turned. "What time should I pick you up?"

Paul felt a shaft of panic. "You're not coming with me?"

Marvin rolled his eyes. "You don't need a wingman for church, Mr. Montrose. Besides, I have arrangements to make for your date."

Paul grasped the door handle with a sweaty hand. You can do this, he told himself. It wasn't the church that made him nervous: it was after. When was the last time he'd asked a woman out? Marvin would know. But that wasn't something he wanted to discuss with his assistant today.

Paul sucked in a breath and thrust open the door. "Come back in about an hour."

Marvin gave him a mock salute. Paul stood in the parking lot and watched until the Escalade was out of sight before turning toward the building.

A white-haired lady shook his hand and thrust a bulletin at him. "Welcome. Service is just starting so you better not dilly-dally."

Paul let himself be ushered into the sanctuary and to a seat near the back. He glanced around for Lauren and spotted her a few rows up and on the opposite side. It gave him a great vantage point to watch her.

Not creepy at all. He was there to focus on his lagging relationship with the Lord, not watch an attractive woman.

Paul enjoyed the music and the order of service printed on the front of the bulletin. It reminded him of the church he'd attended with his parents. He felt a pang of loss. Dad would have been proud to see what Paul had accomplished with the money from his and Mom's life insurance.

"You have a gift, Son," Dad had always told him. "You can turn a few pennies into a few hundred just by touching them."

Paul knew from experience that wasn't literally true. His success was due to hard work and recognizing opportunities. Like the First Upstate Bank. He planned to work with the board of directors to turn the institution around. Once he finished renovating the house on Keuka Lake, he'd commute between there and his penthouse in New York City. Or to the house currently in escrow in Thousand Islands.

The pastor preached from the book of Matthew. "It is easier for a camel to go through the eye of a needle than for a rich man to enter into the kingdom of God."

Paul squirmed on the hard wooden pew. Would his wealth keep him from going to Heaven? That was a difficult truth to swallow.

The pastor read on, "With men this is impossible, but with God all things are possible."

How could he get to heaven? Would he have to give

away everything he'd worked hard for? Paul pulled out his phone and opened the Notes app, tapping a reminder to explore the subject further.

Paul breathed a sigh of relief when the service ended and everyone rose to leave. A few people approached him and shook his hand, welcoming him to their church. Lauren caught his eye, and her face widened into a smile.

Paul's heart expanded as the warmth from her smile filled him with a sense of excitement. It was the same feeling he had when a deal was in process. He watched her weave through chatting groups of two and three people. His breath caught in his throat. She was beautiful, from her mane of brown hair, pulled into a low ponytail, to her flawless skin, down to her open-toed sandals. Her face was void of makeup except for a bit of lip gloss shining from her plump lips.

What was happening to him? The feelings this woman brought up were different from anything he'd felt before.

"Hi," Lauren said, stopping a foot away. "I wondered if you'd actually show up today."

"Of course. We have a lunch date, remember?"

Lauren clasped her hands in front her. Why did she look nervous?

"How could I forget?" she replied.

Paul flipped a hand toward the sanctuary doors. "Ready?"

Lauren nodded and they made their way through the last of the congregation trickling out the doors. Paul spotted Marvin leaning against the passenger side of the Escalade. Taking Lauren's arm, he led her down the concrete ramp to the parking lot.

"There's my assistant. Come on, I'll introduce you."

When they reached the vehicle, Paul introduced Marvin to Lauren. "You've likely seen him in your shop."

"Oh, yes. My assistant prefers to wait on you herself." Lauren sent a smile in Marvin's direction.

Paul felt a shaft of … jealousy? Time to move this conversation along.

"Marvin will drive us to wherever we're going."

"You mean you don't know?" Lauren asked.

"I let Marvin handle those type of details."

They climbed into the back of the SUV. Lauren gave a nervous chuckle. "So, are you like the Lincoln Lawyer or something?"

Paul searched his memory for what she meant by Lincoln Lawyer and came up empty.

Marvin stretched an arm over the passenger seat and turned. "Kind of like that, yeah."

Paul sent him a questioning look.

Marvin laughed. "You need to watch more TV, Mr. Montrose. Or at least pick up a book that isn't about business."

Annoyance fluttered in his chest as Marvin and Lauren exchanged a knowing look.

# Chapter 9

**Lauren ran her** hand down the side of the soft leather seat. What a difference from the scratchy cloth-covered seats in her aging Honda. Whatever Paul did, he must be successful to afford an expensive vehicle like this one.

"What did you think of the service?" she asked.

Paul tapped a finger on his slacks. Lauren noticed the knife-edge pleat in his perfectly pressed khakis. He wore a turquoise golf shirt with a Callaway logo. He'd shed his cardigan before climbing into the car. Lauren glanced sideways, admiring the muscles in his forearm. He had nice hands. Neatly clipped nails and long, tapering fingers.

"It was … interesting."

Lauren half-turned in her seat. "How so?"

"The sermon gave me something to think about."

Lauren sighed. Making conversation for the next hour or so would be difficult. Maybe this whole lunch date thing wasn't the best idea.

She focused on the passing scenery. Soon Marvin turned the Escalade into the Dansville Airport parking lot.

"I didn't know they had a restaurant at the airport,"

she commented.

She caught Marvin's grin in the rearview mirror. "They don't."

He braked to a stop and jumped out to open her door. "After you," he said, waving his hand with a flourish.

Lauren climbed out and glanced around. What was happening?

Paul walked around the back of the SUV. "So, Marvin. What's the plan?"

"Follow me."

Paul took Lauren's arm, and they followed Marvin around the side of an empty hangar and to a plane sitting on the tarmac. The stairs were down, and Lauren's chest rumbled from the throbbing engines.

She pulled her arm from Paul's grasp at the bottom of the steps. A jolt of panic made her breath catch. "Am I being kidnapped?"

Paul looked down with a wrinkled brow. "Kidnapped? No." He shook his head. "Let's go up and see what surprise Marvin has for us." Paul laid a hand on her shoulder. "I'm not in the kidnapping business. Trust me."

There was that killer smile again. Lauren searched Paul's face for any guile and said a quick prayer for guidance. She sensed no creepy vibe and allowed herself to be escorted up the steps and into the plane.

A uniformed woman greeted them at the top. "Welcome. Please come in and take a seat. We'll get in the air shortly."

Lauren's breath caught at the plane's interior. Four seats facing each other, covered in dark leather. Under the windows sat a ledge with cup holders and phone charging plugs.

Paul motioned to her to find a place to sit. Lauren sank onto one of the seats facing the front. Paul sat across from her. Their knees touched and she scooted back to leave a small gap between them.

Marvin spoke quietly to the flight attendant and moved to sit in the first set of seats.

Soon the door closed, and the engine sounds increased in volume.

"What do you think?" Paul asked.

"Of the plane?"

Paul chuckled. "This is a Cessna Citation M2. It is one of the smallest of the Cessna family, with a seating capacity of only seven."

"Do you own this?" Lauren asked, almost afraid of the answer. Who jumps on a plane for a lunch date? Was she being punked, kidnapped, or something else? She wiped sweaty palms down the length of her skirt.

"No. I haven't made that kind of investment yet. I lease the aircraft when I don't feel like riding in the car for an extended distance."

Lauren wracked her brain for an appropriate response. The guy must have serious wealth if he could afford to lease a jet.

The plane jerked forward, and the flight attendance approached. "Please fasten your seatbelts during takeoff. May I get you something to drink?"

Lauren shook her head and struggled to keep her mouth from gaping open.

Paul thanked the woman. "How about a couple of bottles of water."

"Sparkling or regular?"

Paul quirked an eyebrow at Lauren.

"Uh, regular," she answered.

The woman returned a few moments later carrying two frosty bottles.

"Thank you," Lauren said.

Once they were in the air, Lauren leaned forward. "What did you say you do for work?" She hadn't gotten the creep vibe from Paul, but what if he was connected to the Mob or something similar?

Paul opened his water and took a sip. "I invest in real estate. Apartments. A few houses."

Lauren pursed her lips. "You must be very good at it."

Paul didn't answer. Instead, he directed her gaze to the window. "Look down. You can see the Finger Lakes from here."

Lauren pressed her face to the window. Far below, water glistened off the few larger of the eleven Finger Lakes.

"If you look really hard you might be able to see the home I'm renovating on Keuka Lake."

"Where?"

Paul laughed. "Just kidding. You won't see it from here."

Lauren sat back with a huff. She didn't enjoy being the butt of his so-called joke.

"Have you been to Keuka?" Paul asked.

"Sadly, no. I've been to Seneca and Canadaiga."

"I'll have to take you sometime. The lake is breathtaking. My home is right on the water with an amazing view. Did you know Keuka Lake is only three quarters of a mile wide? You can swim the width of it without much effort."

Lauren turned to stare out the window again,

embarrassed over her lack of knowledge of her own state compared to this newcomer. "No, I didn't."

The flight approached their seats. "We'll be landing shortly. Can I get you anything else?"

Lauren stifled a giggle, tempted to ask for caviar and champagne. Wasn't that the snack of choice for the uber-wealthy?

Paul shot her a glance with one raised eyebrow. Lauren shook her head.

"Thank you, Linda. I think we are okay," Paul said.

Linda nodded and returned to her seat.

Paul pulled his phone from the holder along the side of the plane. Lauren took the opportunity to study him. His brown hair curled over his ears and brushed the back of his golf shirt collar. His nose was long and straight and his skin lightly tanned. When he pulled the phone closer to his face, Lauren caught a glimpse of his bicep. The tan line ended at the bottom of the sleeve.

His business must not be all indoors, she mused. Remembering her sister's warning, Lauren asked, "Um, Paul?"

He looked up from his device and held her gaze. "Yes?"

"I, uh, never asked your last name." She bit her lip, hoping he wouldn't take offense.

"You're right. I apologize. Montrose." He stuck out a hand with a grin. "Paul Montrose. Nice to meet you."

Lauren returned his smile. "Lauren Jensen."

"Pleased to meet you."

"Same."

Lauren's hand stayed captive to his warm grip. Butterflies took flight in her empty stomach.

Paul released her hand and cleared his throat.

"Well."

She was saved from answering by the sudden drop in altitude. The runway rose up to meet the plane and soon they were taxiing to a stop. What could possibly be next?

"Thank you, Linda," Paul said as they deplaned. "Ladies first," he said to Lauren, motioning to the open door.

He followed her down the stairs. Lauren stopped at the bottom and turned to look up at him. "Where are we?"

Marvin stood by a waiting vehicle with a smile. "Gabreski Airport."

"Are we eating here?" Lauren asked.

"Although the airport boasts an adequate brew house, I have a feeling Marvin has something a bit more appropriate."

Marvin opened the back door of a waiting limo. "The driver will take you to Fauna Restaurant. I'll wait with the jet."

"Very good. Thank you, Marvin."

Lauren climbed into the limo and Paul followed. She scooted over on the back seat to make room for him. The driver looked over his shoulder.

"Everyone ready?"

Paul glanced at Lauren, eyebrows raised. She nodded.

"Ready."

"I've never ridden in a limousine before," Lauren whispered.

Paul leaned toward her to whisper back. "It's nice."

"It's more than nice." She smoothed her skirt. "It's wonderful. I can't believe I got to ride in a jet and in a limo today."

"I hope lunch isn't a huge letdown."

Her face turned to his with a serious expression. "Why are you doing this, Paul? Are you trying to impress me?"

"Is it working?"

Lauren lowered her lashes. "Yes."

Captivated by her beauty, Paul could only nod. He cleared his throat. "Tell me about your muffin shop. When did you decide that was your career choice."

He felt rather than saw Lauren relax next to him.

"I've always loved to bake." She placed her hands on her stomach. "Pretty obvious, huh?"

Paul laid a hand over one of hers. "Don't do that."

Lauren's gaze swiveled to meet his. "Do what?"

"Make comments about your weight. It isn't healthy."

"Huh. What would you know about it?"

Paul clasped his hands between his knees. He chewed the inside of his cheek before answering. "I know something about being uncomfortable with myself."

"Yeah, sure. I'll bet you never had to worry about calories and metabolism." Lauren turned away to stare out the window.

"As a matter of fact, I recently lost six stones."

Lauren turned back to pin him with narrowed eyes. "What is that in American?"

Paul took in the changeable color of her eyes and the slight smattering of freckles on her nose. A lock of hair had fallen across her cheek. He resisted the urge to brush it behind her ear. This woman enchanted him, and he wasn't sure what to think.

"It's about ninety pounds, give or take."

The sunlight shining through the passing landscape created a strobe-like impression, changing her reflection from light to dark and back again. He could get lost in her unblinking gaze. What would it be like to discover everything about this woman—her dreams, hopes, hurts, and failures. What if he could show her how beautiful she was even though she didn't fit the American ideal of weight and size?

"We're here," announced the limo driver, braking to a stop.

Unfortunate timing.

# Chapter 10

**Lauren hesitated before** stepping out of the limo, hand hovering over the door handle. She looked up at the fancy restaurant marquee and felt a twinge of self-doubt. Was she dressed-up enough for this white tablecloth establishment?

Paul's confession about his past weight struggles caught her off guard. How had he managed to transform himself so drastically while she struggled just to maintain? As usual, the insecurity that hovered came to rest on her shoulders. Sucking in her tummy didn't help.

Paul's warm hand on her back made her feel accepted and worthy to be escorted by such a handsome man. However, she couldn't ignore the stares from other patrons as they entered. They were probably wondering why someone like Paul would be with a frumpy girl like her.

What was he really doing with her? Men didn't usually give her a second glance. Except for one whose name she refused to say out loud, she hadn't been on a date in ages.

Her mother's harsh words echoed in her mind. Men don't want a fat girl. And here she was, with a man who seemed eager to impress her. Was he only trying to impress her enough to sleep with him?

That thought made Lauren's blood boil. She firmly believed in saving her virginity for marriage, even if it meant waiting until she was sixty years old. But was Paul aware of that? Did he see her as nothing more than a conquest?

Despite all these conflicting thoughts, Lauren couldn't deny the fluttering in her stomach whenever she looked at Paul. She wanted to trust him and believe that he saw something special in her, but deep down, doubts still lingered.

The Maître 'd greeted Paul like an old friend. "Mr. Montrose, I have your table ready." He led them to a quiet table near the front window. He pulled out Lauren's chair. Once she was seated, he snapped open the cloth napkin and laid it on her lap.

"Sidney will be along in a moment with waters and to take your drink order," he said with a slight bow.

"Do you know him?" Lauren asked.

Paul shrugged. "No. I assume Marvin told him we were coming."

"Do you let your assistant plan all your dates?"

"Hardly."

Lauren wanted to press him, but a suit-clad waiter appeared at their table with two glasses of water, dripping with condensation.

"Good afternoon. My name is Sidney. May I offer you something besides water?" Another waiter appeared next to Sidney and handed menus to her and Paul.

"I'm okay with water."

"Of course. And for you, sir?"

"I'll have the same. Thank you."

Lauren opened the thick menu and perused the choices. After their brief discussion about weight and weight loss, Lauren felt she should order a salad. But the Scottish Salmon entree called her name.

"Have you had a chance to decide?" Sidney asked when he returned to the table.

Lauren looked across the table at Paul. He met her gaze with raised eyebrows. "Lauren?"

Torn with indecision, she shook her head. "Not yet."

"Give us a moment, would you, please?"

"Of course, sir." Sidney glided away.

"What looks good to you," Paul asked.

Lauren blew out a breath and patted her waist. "Everything. I'm obviously a foodie."

"There go you again." Paul met her gaze with a frown.

Lauren lowered her eyes to the menu. She was used to self-deprecating in regard to her weight, but Paul seemed to have an issue with her mentioning it. He probably didn't want the reminder of how he'd asked a fat girl out. Best to get this date over and get home.

Paul folded the menu and laid it on the edge of the table. "I'm going to have the Classic Fish and Chips. It will be interesting to see how it compares with London fare."

How did he maintain his weight? Fish and chips weren't exactly low on the calorie and carb scale.

She laid her menu on his.

"Have you decided, then?" Paul asked.

Lauren nodded. "The salmon."

Sidney was back at their table. "Good choice,

madame. And for you?"

"Fish and chips. Thank you. And would you bring us each a mimosa?"

"Of course, Mr. Montrose. Are we celebrating today?"

Paul's gaze was warm when his eyes met hers. "Our first date. The first of many, I hope."

Lauren felt a thrill go through her, then a shaft of alarm.

This was moving too fast. What was Paul's end game? A jet ride, limo, and ridiculously expensive lunch. Did he hope to soften her up with champagne and … what? He seemed the perfect gentleman. But so had what's his name. Until she let him know she wouldn't spend the night with him in New York City at his five-star hotel.

His parting words still stung like a thousand needles.

"I don't want to see you naked, anyway," he'd spat. His words were eerily similar to her mother's. "You're too fat."

Paul watched several emotions move across Lauren's face.

"What are you thinking?" he asked.

Her smile looked forced when she answered. "It doesn't matter."

It did matter. To him. He wanted to get to know this woman. Why was she so focused on her size? Who had convinced her that it mattered? He knew what it was like to be judged by appearance.

It wasn't until his health scare Paul decided to make changes to his sedentary lifestyle. Heavy meals and no exercise had gifted him with high cholesterol and blood pressure that was approaching a dangerous level.

But Lauren? She'd never be the size he'd been. He found her curves alluring rather than off-putting.

"I'm a foodie too," Paul said. "I find that I must be cognizant of how I approach my daily diet. For instance, after this lunch, I won't eat again until tomorrow."

Lauren smiled and it lit up her face.

Paul continued, "Perhaps another muffin for breakfast."

She chuckled. "Perhaps not. I'm closed on Sundays and Mondays."

Paul feigned outrage. "That is not acceptable. How will I survive without my pumpkin muffin?"

"You mean half a muffin."

Paul felt his face grow warm. "Indeed."

Lauren placed her elbows on the table and leaned forward. "Why do you toss half your muffin in the trash?"

"Well, I ..."

"Yes?" She tapped a finger on the table. "I'm waiting."

"As I mentioned in the car, I recently lost a significant amount of weight. I can't justify eating an entire baked good in one sitting."

Lauren leaned back. "Hm. I guess that makes sense. So, I don't have to be insulted?"

"Heavens, no."

"You could take the other half in a to go box," Lauren suggested.

"But then I wouldn't have an excuse to come back the next day, now would I?"

It was Lauren's turn to blush. Paul loved watching her face turn pink. He congratulated himself on saying the right thing.

Sidney returned and gave them each a glass of mimosa. His tray also held two small plates with a green salad.

"Here you go. Your entrees will be out soon."

Paul held up his mimosa glass. "Here's to the beginning of a great friendship."

"I don't normally drink," Lauren said. She grasped the stem of the glass and clicked it gently to his. "But I'll have a few sips."

Paul watched her face as she took a tentative sip of the cold orange juice mixed with champagne.

"Well?" he asked.

"I like it."

"Good. I want today to be perfect."

They ate their salads in silence. When they finished and pushed the plates aside, a waiter took the plates and forks away, then used a small brush to tidy the tablecloth.

Lauren giggled. When he'd finished, she said, "I've never seen anyone do that."

Paul laughed with her. "It's like having a maid follow you around."

"I wouldn't know."

Her phone dinged and Lauren dug in her purse to glance at it. "Sorry. It's my sister. She wants to know how it's going."

"How is it going?" Paul wanted to know.

Lauren pretended to think, tapping the phone

against her lips. "I'd give it a solid seven so far."

Paul slapped a hand on his cheek. "Only a seven?"

"I'll reconsider after I've tasted the salmon."

Paul laughed, delighted at her sense of humor. "I hope to get at least a nine point five."

"Whew. That's a pretty tall order." She tapped something on her phone and returned it to her purse.

Paul struggled to find a conversation starter. He desperately wanted to know what Lauren had responded to her sister.

"Tell me about your sister," he said.

# Chapter 11

Lauren felt her face tighten. She loved her sister to death, but she didn't want Sam's intrusion into her lunch date. Although she enjoyed basking in the attention Sam brought when they were together, part of her resented it. Once Sam was in the picture, Lauren faded into the background.

She was saved from answering by the arrival of their entrees.

"This looks great," Lauren said, sniffing the steam rising from the salmon.

"Agreed," Paul said, inhaling with closed eyes. "Mind if I say grace?"

"Oh, uh, sure." That was unexpected. But nice.

Paul said a short prayer of thanks for the food and for the beautiful day. Lauren echoed his 'amen.'

She forked a piece of fish and brought the fork to her mouth. "This is yummy," she said with a groan.

Paul didn't seem embarrassed to pick up one of the pieces of fish with his fingers. He took a bite. "This is good."

"As good as London?"

Paul chewed with a thoughtful look on his face. "I'm going to give it a solid nine out of ten."

Lauren giggled. "I'm giving this salmon a perfect ten." She took another sip of the mimosa, deciding she liked it. Not that she was against drinking in general. But alcohol tended to add calories she couldn't afford.

But today was a cheat day. She'd pay for it with salads for the next two days.

The conversation during the rest of the meal consisted of dissecting the various flavors and textures of their food. Lauren enjoyed every minute of their discussion. She'd finally met someone as passionate about food as she was. Unlike that other guy who thought it boring to talk about food.

Was Paul too good to be true?

Both declined dessert. Paul ordered cappuccinos instead.

"In case I forget, thank you for lunch," Lauren said, sipping the piping hot coffee.

"My pleasure. I'm glad you enjoyed it."

"You said you'd tell me how you know Chandler Daniels," Lauren said.

Paul leaned back in his chair. "Ah, yes. Mr. Daniels." He took a sip of coffee. "We are working on a business deal together."

"How did you meet?"

A waiter arrived and discreetly placed a leather folder on the table. Paul set his cup down. Opening the folder, her studied the bill.

Lauren tried to sneak a look at the total, but Paul's long fingers covered the receipt as he signed his name with a flourish.

Before Lauren could push back her chair, Paul was up and helping her stand. He again placed his hand on the small of her back to guide her to the door. The warmth of his hand spread down to her toes. She'd missed this. The feeling of being pampered. Special. Having the full attention of an attractive man. Would this end the same way as her ex, with tears and regret?

Stop overthinking, she told herself. Enjoy the moment.

The limo sat idling in front of the restaurant. How did the driver know the exact moment they'd be finished? Must be some unspoken rich thing. She climbed in and slid over to make room for Paul.

After they'd boarded the jet for the ride home, Lauren's eyes grew heavy.

"Recline your seat," Paul said, showing her how the controls worked.

Her lids dropped and she felt someone lay a soft blanket over her. The bump of the plane hitting the runway jolted her out of a cozy dream.

She opened her eyes to find Paul grinning at her.

"Did I snore?" she asked, alarmed that she'd managed to embarrass herself.

"No, but you smiled in your sleep. Must have been a good dream."

Lauren rubbed her cheeks to wake up. "I don't remember." But she did remember. She'd been on a boat with Paul, and he'd leaned forward to kiss her. Before their lips touched the boat hit a wave and jerked them apart. That must have been the plane hitting the tarmac. Her face grew warm.

Paul reached over to help her bring her seat to an upright position. "Are you all right?"

"Y-yes. Fine." She wasn't fine. What she needed to do was get off this plane, go home, and gather her jumbled thoughts.

Paul studied her face. "Let's get you back to your car."

Drat. Her car was still parked at the church. She had to endure one more ride next to this guy who must have an ulterior motive for impressing her with his wealth. Insecurity roared its ugly head and all she could think about was why a good-looking millionaire would pay more than a nanosecond of attention to someone like her.

Marvin held open the door of the SUV. Paul walked to the other side and climbed in. Lauren heaved a sigh of relief when Marvin pulled into the church. Her car sat like an abandoned kitten in the middle of the parking lot. Before the Escalade came to a complete stop, Lauren had opened the door.

"Thank you for a nice day," she said, leaning down to address Paul. "I had a good time."

Lauren swung the door closed before he could respond. Heat from the interior of her sedan hit her when she climbed in. After cranking up the A/C, she drove out of the lot and pointed her car toward Hornell.

What was she thinking, spending the day with some guy she didn't know? What if he wasn't what he appeared? What ifs swirled in her brain on the twenty-minute drive to town.

Her phone pinged with an incoming text. At the stoplight at the Walmart, she glanced at the phone to see a text from Samantha.

Call me - no hurry

Sam would have to wait. First, pick Molly up from Kennedy's. Second, spend hours obsessing over Paul and his possible motives. Third, dissect every bit of conversation and nuance. A distant fourth was to pray.

Paul stepped out of the Escalade, intending to say something to Lauren before she practically spun out of the parking lot in her little car. He climbed into the front seat and fixed his gaze on Marvin's confused face.

"What just happened?" Paul asked.

"I thought the lady had a good time. Up until she woke up from her nap, that is. Did you say something to her?"

Paul thought back to the plane's landing. "I don't believe so."

"Hm." Marvin pulled out of the church parking lot onto Highway 36 toward Hornell.

Paul stared at the passing scenery. Rows upon rows of corn fields waved in the breeze. A few birds circled and dove, hunting for mice or voles.

What did he do wrong? He'd wanted to ask for Lauren's phone number. Sure, he could easily get it from the bank's system, but that might seem creepy.

"I'm a total plonker," Paul said aloud.

Marvin laughed. "Who can understand the mind of a woman?"

"Not I," Paul said, shaking his head.

His phone rang while they were on the road. The vehicle's Bluetooth picked it up.

"It's John Druban. I've set a tee time for Tuesday at ten. Will that work for you?"

Paul sent a questioning look in Marvin's direction. The man had an uncanny ability to memorize Paul's calendar. Marvin nodded.

"That sounds brilliant."

"Great. I'll text you the address of the course."

They disconnected.

"I'll add it to your calendar," Marvin said.

"Thanks. And while you're at it, please see if Ian is available to fly up tonight."

"Your golf pro?"

"The same. Maybe we can get a quick round in tomorrow before I play with the men on Tuesday."

"Gotcha."

Paul drummed his fingers on the arm rest. One of the advantages of having money was being able to summon people to assist him at any time. Ian would no doubt jump at the chance to travel from Florida and spend a couple days in New York.

"Tell Ian I'll put him up at 142. And if he can get here tonight, tell him I'll throw in dinner at Jean-Georges."

"Sure thing. I'll take care of it."

Paul leaned his head back, confident Marvin would arrange for the Cessna to pick up Ian and deliver him to one of the New York airports. And all the other arrangements for getting Ian to and from The City out here to rural upstate New York.

When they arrived at the rental, Paul went immediately to the kitchen. Nothing like a little food creation to relieve the stress of wondering what he'd said or done to Lauren to make her take flight.

"I'm going to my room," Marvin said, loosening his tie.

Paul waved him off, already studying the contents of the refrigerator.

Forty minutes later, Paul poured himself a glass of Cabernet and took in the sight of his creation. Seared slices of Filet mixed with red and green bell peppers, onion, garlic, and a smidge of ginger.

"Smells delicious," Marvin said, stepping into the kitchen. He'd changed into loose sweats and kicked off his black dress shoes.

Paul waved his wine glass. "Can I pour you a glass?"

Marvin grinned. "Mr. Montrose, you know I don't drink. But I will take some of that—whatever that is."

"I'm sorry, you probably didn't get lunch, did you?"

Marvin reached into the cupboard for a plate. "Linda and I ate on the plane."

Paul quirked an eyebrow. "Linda? And you?"

Marvin shrugged. "She's a nice lady. I hated to see her hang out all afternoon alone."

"Whatever," Paul said with a wry smile.

"You figure out what you did wrong with the muffin lady?"

"Sadly, no." Now he'd have to wait two days to talk to her. At least he had something to look forward to. Ian's arrival and a golf match on Tuesday.

# Chapter 12

**Lauren yawned and** stretched, enjoying the two extra hours of sleep. Although missing the income from closing on Monday, she had an extra day to catch up on sleep, bookkeeping, and housework.

She stretched her legs out on the sofa and leisurely sipped her second cup of coffee. Perhaps she'd stay in her PJs until noon. Then she'd work on her finances. But not yet.

Her phone buzzed. A text from Samantha.

Are you awake?

Lauren frowned. She'd forgotten about Sam's text yesterday. She hit Sam's name on the Favorites screen and waited for Sam to pick up.

Sam's voice screeched through the phone. "You went out with Paul Montrose?"

Lauren held the phone away from her ear and put it on speaker. "Calm down, Sam."

"Don't tell me to calm down! You went out with Paul Freaking Montrose?"

"Yeah, so?"

"So he has his own Wikipedia page. Did you know that?"

Lauren reached for her mug on the coffee table.

"Huh?"

"Oh, good grief, Lauren. Don't you know anything?"

"Apparently not. What are you talking about?" Lauren stood and shuffled to the kitchen to refill her mug.

Sam's sigh was like wind blowing through the tiny speaker. "Paul Montrose was just named the youngest billionaire in the United States by Forbes Magazine. How could you not know this?"

Lauren's hand shook and coffee dribbled onto the counter. "Are you sure we're talking about the same guy?"

"One sec and I'll send you the magazine cover."

Lauren heard the click and waited for Sam's text. The photo came through a little blurry, but there it was. She inhaled just as she took a sip of coffee. Bad timing. She coughed until her eyes watered.

Sam's voice echoed in the tiny kitchen. "Are you all right?"

Lauren waved a hand in front of her face. "I'm fine." She studied the magazine cover. Yup, that was Paul. The man she'd spent yesterday with. Who flew on a jet. And had a personal driver. Holy cow. With that kind of money, he could have any woman he wanted. So why her?

"Tell me about your date. Every single detail."

Lauren blew out a breath. "I need a moment to process." She carried her mug back to the living room and sank onto the sofa. Molly padded over and rested her chin on Lauren's knee.

"First, you have to tell me how this all came about," Sam said.

Lauren thought back to her conversation with Paul at the YMCA. "I bumped into him at the Y—"

"Had you met him before?"

"He came into the shop a couple times." She left out the part about Molly jumping on him and the subsequent coffee dumped on his suit.

"Okay, go on. This is so cool. My sister is dating a billionaire."

"No, no, no. I am not dating him. We went out one time."

"Yeah, but he'll ask you out again. I know it."

"Sam, let's be honest. If he's that rich, he won't want to be with me."

Sam's voice was stern when she replied, "Stop. Any man would love to have you for a girlfriend. You are fun, funny, and a wonderful cook."

Lauren shook her head. "What about, you know . . ."

Sam laughed. "That loser? He's history, and he didn't deserve you."

Lauren's eyes prickled with tears. "He said I was fat."

There was silence from Sam's end. Then, "He was stupid. You are not fat. You're beautiful."

Lauren sniffled. "Yeah, in a 'you have a beautiful face but a fat body' type of beautiful."

Samantha sighed. "You've been listening to Mom, haven't you?"

Lauren couldn't answer.

"Sis, let that go for a minute and tell me about your date. Please. I need some distraction."

"Why, has that stalker contacted you again?"

"No. But it still makes me nervous. Come on, give

me details, girl."

"Fine." Lauren told Samantha about the plane ride, the limo, and the restaurant. Sam pressed her for details about Paul. What was he like? Was he funny, serious, sarcastic? What did they order?

"Are you trying to live vicariously through me?" Lauren asked with a chuckle.

"How can you tell? Frankly, I haven't been out on a date for months. By the time I get home after a photo shoot, I'm beat."

"Sucks to be you," Lauren said.

"For sure. When are you going out again?"

Lauren shrugged, though Samantha couldn't see her. "I don't know."

"Did he ask for your number?"

Lauren's face grew warm. She'd dashed out of the car so quickly Paul hadn't had a chance to say a word. "No."

"But he knows where to find you. Watch, he'll be back in the Muffin Top tomorrow morning, pretending to be a customer. If he's interested, he'll get your number then."

"Whatever, Sis. I really don't have time to date. Between the shop and working with Molly, I'm busy."

"Lauren, if Paul Montrose, youngest billionaire in the history of the world, wants your number, you give it to him. Do you hear me?"

Lauren sighed. "Fine. But don't hold your breath."

They exchanged 'love yous' and disconnected. Lauren tapped the phone against her cheek. Why would someone that rich be interested in her? That was the question that plagued her the rest of the morning.

Paul woke early and padded to the kitchen for a cup of his special imported tea. While it brewed, he went in search of his assistant. Marvin's door was cracked, and he'd scrawled some words on a stickie note.

'Back shortly. Ran to the store for some eggs'

Paul smiled. What would he do without Marvin?

He added a dollop of cream to the stout tea and carried his cup outside to the porch. The view couldn't have been more different from his penthouse in New York City. Green rolling hills and acres of tilled farmland contrasted with concrete and steel structures in New York City. In The City, Paul rarely sat on the balcony. The view from there was uninspiring. Row after row of high rises, the only sunlight was reflected in their windows.

But here, the morning sun warmed his shoulders and filled him with a new sense of purpose. Hornell reminded him of his parents' home in England. His thoughts turned to the house he was having renovated on Keuka Lake. Would it be the place he could finally call home? Would the loneliness that dogged him since his parents' death finally ease?

Mum and Dad had been gone for two years, and he still missed them like crazy. Paul wanted what his folks had. A long and happy marriage. Kids. Speaking of which, what was his ne'er-do-well brother up to? Nigel hadn't contacted him in weeks, which was unusual. To say they were opposites was an understatement. Thinking about Nigel soured his mood. He'd likely crawl up from some cesspool and ask for more money.

And pile on the guilt when Paul told him no.

Nigel knew every button to push, and he did so without hesitation. Which is why Paul eventually caved in. Nigel knew he would, and Paul knew he knew. His stomach churned with suppressed anger.

Paul's thoughts were interrupted by tires crunching on the gravel drive. He stood and carried his cup down the steps and around to the front of the house. Marvin was climbing out of the SUV when Paul reached the driveway.

"Morning, Mr. Montrose." Marvin waved the reusable shopping bag. "Bought some eggs and a few other things."

"Well done." Paul followed his assistant into the house and refilled his mug with hot water from the electric kettle. "I'll go shower. Let's leave in forty-five minutes." Hopefully that would shake off his bad temper.

"Are we stopping at the Muffin Top this morning?"

Paul answered without turning. "The shop is closed on Monday." He felt Marvin's gaze boring into his back.

"That's a darn shame," Marvin muttered.

Yes, it was. A glimpse of Lauren might shake him out of the black mood hovering over him like a sodden blanket.

After a quick shower, Paul reached into the closet for the suit Marvin had cleaned after the coffee spill. He pulled off the plastic covering and frowned.

"Marvin," he shouted. "Get in here!"

Marvin strode into the bedroom. "What is it?"

Paul stabbed a finger at the suit jacket. "You said this was cleaned. Clearly, it has not. Did you even look at the jacket?"

Marvin took a step back. "Well, I—"

Paul's ire rose as he took in the slight dark area on the suit front, contrasting with the lighter blue shade of the fabric. "This is—was—my favorite suit. Now it's ruined. You should have checked to see if the cleaners had done their job before picking it up. Can't you do anything right?"

Marvin's face tightened. "Sorry, Mr. Montrose. It won't happen again." He spun on his heels and strode from the bedroom.

Paul sank onto the king-sized bed, wishing he could take back his words. What had gotten into him? Why was he letting a ruined suit upset him? Because of his half-brother.

The two cups of strong tea churned in his stomach. He owed Marvin an apology. His quick temper had gotten the best of him on more than one occasion. But never had it been directed at his assistant. He needed to fix this. And fast.

Paul shoved the ruined suit into the far corner of the walk-in closet and picked out a dark gray sports coat and golf slacks. Instead of his usual white button-down shirt, he chose a light mauve golf shirt. If everything went the way it was supposed to, Ian would arrive later in the day for a quick review of Paul's golf swing.

He found Marvin sitting in the Escalade, one hand on the steering wheel and the other resting on the windowsill. Sunglasses hid his eyes. Marvin frowned when Paul climbed into the front seat, something he rarely did.

Marvin started the vehicle and put it into reverse.

Paul cleared his throat. "Uh, Marvin, I—"

"Where to, Mr. Montrose?"

Marvin was not going to make this easy. Very well, then. "I'm sorry. What I said to you was unconscionable and I dearly regret it."

Marvin shoved the SUV into Park and lowered his sunglasses to glare at him. "Yes, it was." He turned to face out the windshield, shoving his glasses up. "Don't do it again."

For a moment, Paul was tempted to respond, "Who's the employer here?" But he held his tongue.

"I won't. Please forgive me." Paul held his breath. If Marvin quit, Paul would be sunk.

"Fine. But get out of my space." Marvin hooked a thumb over his shoulder toward the back seat.

Paul climbed out of the front passenger seat and into the back. Still testing the waters, he said, "Did Ian arrive last night?"

"Yes. I've arranged for him to catch the jet at La Guardia and land in Dansville. I'll pick him up and take him straight to Twin Hickory Golf Club."

"Very good. Thank you."

"Oh, and he said he was bringing a friend. He didn't mention if his friend was male or female."

Paul caught the ghost of a smile in Marvin's rearview mirror reflection.

"Knowing Ian, probably a woman."

"I got an email from the Air B&B. He might be interested in selling if the offer was right."

Paul rubbed a hand across his face. It might be convenient to own the house where he and Marvin were staying. It would be handy if he had to return to the bank once he'd done what he planned to make the institution profitable again.

"Contact our real estate attorney at Pearson Hardman and ask him to have an agent run some comps. And contact an appraiser as well. And a home inspector. Let's get the ball rolling."

"Will do."

"How's the punch list coming on the Keuka house remodel?"

"Pretty good. I think you should head over there this weekend and have a look. I think you'll be pleased."

Paul nodded. He'd ask Lauren if she would like to take a drive next weekend to see the house. If she was still interested, that is. The way she'd bolted out of the vehicle yesterday still rankled. Had he done or said something to upset her?

As his father used to tell him, you won't know unless you ask.

# Chapter 13

**Lauren leaned down** to scratch between Molly's ears before standing. She rose on tiptoes and stretched her arms up, twisting right and left.

"Lounging time is over, Molly girl. Time to dive into paperwork."

After quick romp with the pup in her yard, Lauren opened her laptop and pulled up her banking website.

"No, no, no!" she said, viewing her bank balance. "How can I be overdrawn?" Her stomach twisted as she reviewed the most recent transactions.

"I've been hacked."

She punched in the bank's phone number with trembling fingers.

"Carol, can you look at my account?" she asked when Carol answered. "I think I've been hacked."

"Oh, no, Lauren. Let me check. Oh, yes, I see. There are several transactions on your debit card. I assume you haven't been to Ohio in the last couple of days?"

"Of course not." Except for going with Paul to Westhampton Beach, she hadn't been out of Hornell for weeks.

"You'll need to come down and fill out an affidavit

of fraudulent activity."

Lauren could barely speak. "When can I get my money back?"

"Once you fill out the form and I submit it to our fraud department, you should have provisional credit within forty-eight hours."

"Provisional credit?"

"We will return the money into your account on a provisional basis until the investigation is complete. Once the fraud department determines you didn't, in fact, make those debit card transactions, you'll have full use of the funds."

"But that money is mine! I didn't use my card in Ohio."

"I understand. The first thing is to get the form filled out and submitted. When can you come down to the bank?"

Lauren glanced around her tiny kitchen. Nothing had changed in the room, but her world had just shifted. "I'll be there in less than an hour."

"Great. May I suggest you also check your credit cards? If someone has stolen your identity, they may have gotten access to your social security number too."

Lauren disconnected and lowered her head into her hands. This couldn't be happening. How could her identity have been stolen? She'd been super careful not to use unsecured WiFi connections or shop on questionable websites. Holding her breath, Lauren logged on to her credit card account.

A burst of adrenaline shot from her head to her fingertips. The card she used for business was maxed out. A search of her credit history revealed three new credit accounts opened within the past few days.

How could this be happening? Lauren shoved her chair back and paced the small apartment. What should she do first? How would she be able to sustain her small business if her identity was stolen?

Tears filled her eyes. Being a small business owner was difficult enough without having this happen. But first, go to the bank and fill out the forms.

Paul stopped at the new accounts desk. "Carol, I'm going to be gone most of the afternoon. I emailed you a letter to send to the board members. Would you take a look at it and make sure it sounds okay? If so, please forward it to the board."

Carol stared up at him with a frown. Was he asking too much of her? Carol wasn't his assistant. After his misstep with Marvin that morning, he should be more sensitive.

"If you have time, that is," Paul added. He held his breath, waiting for Carol to respond.

"Sure. I have a customer coming in to fill out an affidavit of fraudulent activity. That might take some time. We'll have to close her account and cancel the debit card. And open a new account."

Paul tapped a finger on Carol's computer monitor. "When you have time, then." He turned to leave and stopped. "Thank you for all your help, Carol. I do appreciate it."

Carol beamed under his praise and Paul breathed a sigh of relief. He'd have to make more of an effort to show his appreciation to the staff. Sometimes he got so focused on business he forgot about the people he worked with. His employees had raved over the muffins Marvin had brought in on Friday. Paul spoke into his voice memo app. "Ask Marvin to place a regular weekly muffin order for the staff." He forwarded the memo to his assistant.

Marvin pulled up to the curb in front of the bank and Paul climbed in. He shed his sport coat and slipped off his dress shoes and socks. Marvin had placed a pair of short socks and his golf shoes on the floor behind the driver's seat.

"Thanks, Marvin," Paul said as he donned the shoes and socks.

"Ian and his lady friend are already at the golf course."

Paul smiled. 'Lady friend,' indeed. Who was a worse womanizer, Ian or Marvin?

He stared out the window as the car wound its way up the road to the golf course. A few puffy clouds hovered over the distant hills. What a breathtaking vista. Paul took in the neat rows of crops climbing resembling a patchwork quilt of shades of green and gold. He'd never tire of the sight. When the Keuka Lake house was complete, he'd be happy to stay here in Upstate New York and limit his visits to The City.

New York City boasted world-class restaurants and delightful theatre productions. And shopping? Oh, yes. Furs, diamonds, custom-made clothing. New York offered it all. But Paul had not found satisfaction in living in the impersonal hustle of The City.

He longed for a place where people might recognize him on the street and say hello. Where he could be a regular at a restaurant or . . . a muffin shop?

Perhaps it was time to slow the pace of growth of

his empire and focus on settling down. Finding what his parents had—lasting love and commitment to another. He ran a mental checklist though the few women he'd met in New York and London. Frankly, they'd been more interested in his wealth that in him.

Except Lauren. She seemed unaware of the Forbes writeup. That had garnered way too much attention. Unwanted attention. Suddenly women—and men— who'd never glanced his way and wanted to be friends. And more than friends.

Investment opportunities, parties on yachts, meetings with movers and shakers.

Paul studied his hands, gripped in his lap. Being able to turn dross into gold was both a blessing and a curse.

# Chapter 14

Paul climbed out of the SUV and took a moment to stretch before ambling toward the unimpressive pro shop. It looked a bit like an abandoned building. No signage indicated the entrance nor directed golfers where to check in. The disappointing ambiance did not distract from the one hundred eighty-degree view from the first hole. Paul breathed in a lungful of fresh air.

"Beautiful," he said.

His golf pro, Ian, approached in a golf cart, accompanied by a striking young woman wearing a pink golf shirt and matching pink visor. As she climbed out of the cart, Paul took a moment to admire her tanned legs.

"Paul, my man!" Ian grabbed Paul in a firm handshake and pulled him in for a bro hug.

Paul stiffened, still uncomfortable to these Americans and their exuberant greetings.

Ian seemed unaffected by Paul's lack of response. "Thanks for inviting me up to work on your game. This is my friend, Heather Cole."

Paul shook Heather's hand, taking notice of her polished pink fingernails.

"Nice to meet you," Heather said.

"Same." Paul sent a questioning glance to his grinning golf pro.

"Heather is working on qualifying for the LPGA," Ian said. "I didn't think you'd mind if she tagged along on today's outing."

Paul struggled to hide his annoyance. He'd hoped for Ian's undivided attention to prepare him for tomorrow with the local men. It wouldn't do to be humiliated on the course.

"Let's get on with it," Paul said.

By the time they'd completed eighteen holes, Paul was more than ready to see the backside of Ian and his 'friend.' They'd been handsy the entire time. Ian made a point to stand behind Heather, either directing her swing with his body pressed against hers or with his hands on her shoulders.

Marvin was already waiting by the Escalade when they returned the golf carts. Paul directed Heather to sit in the front while he and Ian climbed into the back.

Ian slapped Paul on the knee. "Thanks again for having me up here."

Paul grumbled a response.

"How long you going to be up here in the sticks?" Ian asked.

"Not long."

"Long enough to kick those local guys' butts?"

Paul ran a hand through his hair. "Sure." He leaned forward and spoke to Marvin. "Drop me at the rental, would you?"

Marvin caught his eye in the rearview mirror. "Sure thing."

To Ian, Paul said, "Marvin will take you to the

Dansville airport for your ride back to The City."

The rest of the ride was blissfully quiet. When they pulled up to the Air B&B, Paul climbed out. He leaned into the vehicle and reached out to shake Ian's hand. "Thanks for coming."

To Marvin, he said, "After you've dropped them off, please come back and take me to the bank."

Marvin gave him a mock salute and pulled away.

Paul had enough time to shower and dress in a suit before Marvin returned.

"Remind me to find a new golf pro," Paul said.

He appreciated Marvin's lack of response.

"Let Ian know he will be returning to Florida tonight," Paul added.

"Yes, sir."

Marvin pulled to a stop in front of the bank and Paul climbed out of the SUV.

"I'll text you when I'm ready to go home. Or I may walk. I don't know yet." Blowing off some steam would be a good idea before that steam blew in the wrong direction. He'd already offended his assistant. Better to not offend anyone else today.

"Mr. Montrose—Paul, I have a form for you to sign," Carol said as he strode into the bank.

He halted in front of the new accounts desk and held out his hand.

"Oh, I already put it on your desk," Carol said.

Paul closed his eyes and prayed for patience. "And if I hadn't made it back today? Would you have left it on my desk overnight?"

Carol's inhaled breath sounded like a gasp. "Of course not."

Paul pinched the bridge of his nose. "All right.

Thank you."

Carol dropped her gaze to her computer. Great, he'd done it again. He was two-for-two today.

His office was a welcome respite from Carol's stiff posture. After logging onto his computer, Paul pulled the paperwork toward him.

Affidavit Of Fraudulent Transactions read the bold black print at the top. He scanned the document and slowed down to read every word.

Lauren Jensen, DBA Muffin Top Bakery had over a thousand dollars stolen from her account, which was currently overdrawn.

He sprang from his chair and strode to Carol's desk. "Who approves the overdrafts here?" he demanded.

"Usually Margie," Carol said with a worried frown.

Paul tapped her desk with the forms. "Usually?"

"I sometimes do it if she is sick."

Paul let out an exasperated breath. "Who did the report today?"

"Margie."

He glanced across the lobby but didn't see the operations supervisor at her desk. "Can you see if Ms. Jensen's overdrafts were approved today?"

Carol tapped on her keyboard for what seemed like ten minutes while Paul waited. He wasn't sure what to expect. If her overdrafts were paid, the bank stood to lose money. But if the charges were returned … Before Paul could complete the thought, Carol looked up.

"The transactions were all done using the debit card on file. Therefore, they were automatically paid. Her account is now overdrawn."

Paul blew out a breath. "I assume our policy is to reverse the insufficient funds charges."

"Of course. And I opened a new account for Lauren today. Once our fraud department receives the document, she'll get provisional credit in twenty-four to forty-eight hours."

"I'm well aware of the banking rules." Paul grabbed a pen from Carol's desk and signed the affidavit. "Let's get this submitted ASAP."

Carol's mouth tightened. She picked up the forms and stood, taking them to the copier.

Paul returned to his office and sank onto the plush chair. Would it be an invasion of privacy to get Lauren's phone number from the bank records?

Probably.

He logged off the computer and walked across the lobby to where Carol stood scanning the forms. "I'll be gone the rest of the afternoon," he said.

Carol barely glanced at him. "Fine."

Lauren's phone buzzed with an incoming text from her long-time friend, Mike.

I have your mug board ready. I'm outside your shop
**Lauren**: Awesome! I'll be down in 2 min

Finally, a bright spot in an otherwise rotten day.

'Come on, Molly, let's go down and see Mike's creation."

Molly leaped up from her bed and wagged her tail as she watched her dog-mom slip into a pair of white sneakers.

Lauren used the inside stairs to the bakery kitchen, cutting through the room and into the dining area. She spied Mike outside unloading a wooden peg board from his ancient pickup.

She unlocked the front door and held it open while Mike tilted the board sideways to fit through the door.

"Where do you want it?"

"I have just the place for it." Lauren pointed to a space where the display case jutted up against a bare wall.

"I'll be right back with my tools."

Lauren stayed out of the way as Mike measured, leveled, and drilled holes to mount the peg board. He'd stenciled across the top 'Take A Mug, Leave A Mug.'

"It's perfect, Mike," Lauren gushed. "Thank you."

"Happy to do it."

She stood back and admired Mike's handiwork. The board took up most of the empty wall. Lauren thought it might be fun for her regulars to bring their own coffee mugs and hang them up. She'd save a bit of money on disposable cups and also help the environment.

"How you gonna keep people from using someone else's mug?"

Lauren grinned. "Got it covered." She went to the kitchen and returned waving a label gun. "I'll let customers pick their spot and label it."

"Great idea." He leaned down to pet Molly. "How's my girl?" Molly rewarded Mike with a sloppy kiss. He wiped his mouth as he straightened.

"How much do I owe you?" Lauren asked.

Mike shrugged again, his shoulders hunching against the faded tee. If only she'd fallen for this guy instead of the one that broke her heart. She and Samantha and Mike had been inseparable in high school, even though Sam was two grades behind them. Mike still carried a torch for Sam, but she didn't like him that way.

Mike smoothed his beard. "Let's see, labor and materials …. I guess it's good for a couple dozen muffins."

"Oh, come on, Mike. At least let me pay you for the materials." Although how she'd pay him was beyond her ability to fathom. Until the bank credited her money, she was broker than broke.

"I'll send you a bill," Mike said as he gathered his tools.

Lauren pressed her lips together. She'd smother her pride today. But she'd find a way to make it up to him. She followed him outside and waited while he loaded his tool bag into the back of the truck and slammed the tailgate.

"Thanks again, Mike." Lauren reached for her friend and pulled him in for a hug.

Mike's arms were warm around her thin tank top. She let him hold her for a few moments before pulling away.

If only things were different. She and Mike would have made the perfect couple. Small-town born and raised and not eager to leave. With a sigh, Lauren watched him drive off with a wave of his arm through the open window.

Glancing down the street, she spied Paul striding toward her with a murderous scowl.

# Chapter 16

**Irritation still chafed** like a pebble in his shoe as Paul walked from the bank to Lauren's bakery. Perhaps the process of putting one foot in front of the other would calm his nerves.

That didn't happen.

His blood pressure rose when he spied Lauren hugging some lumberjack-looking guy outside her shop. He caught up to her before she slipped inside the bakery.

"Who was that?" He came to a halt and her mutt sniffed his pant leg. He shoved the animal away with one foot.

Lauren whirled to face him. "Excuse me?"

"Who was that guy you were hugging?"

An angry red flush rose from Lauren's chest to her forehead. "That's none of your business." She moved toward the shop door, the dog close on her heels.

"I would think it is my business. When I take a woman out, it's with the understanding that I won't find her embracing some other man the next day." He regretted the words the minute they flew from his mouth. What a plonker. Or in American, what a horse's ass.

Fire shot from Lauren's eyes. Paul fully expected to see steam coming from her ears. She stood legs apart and arms akimbo.

"I don't know who you think you are, Mr. Forbes Magazine cover model. But your money does not give you the right to dictate who I hug and when I hug someone."

Paul's stomach sank. She'd seen that blasted magazine cover. He raised a hand in surrender. "You're right. I'm an idiot."

Some of the starch seemed to come out of her. Surprisingly, tears formed in her eyes and a few dripped down her cheeks. Buggers. Angry women were one thing. But ones that dripped moisture were way out of his league.

Lauren wiped them away with an angry swipe. "I've had a very bad day."

He followed her into the shop. She shoved the door closed and leaned back against the counter. Paul longed to pull her to him, but he didn't want to risk a punch in the eye.

"Why are you here, anyway?"

"I, uh, needed some air." He couldn't mention the fraud on her account without breaking some banking privacy regulation. "I saw you and I thought … Well, it doesn't matter what I thought." He blew out a breath. "Anyway, what's this?" he asked, motioning toward the pegboard.

Lauren's face held the ghost of a smile. "That's my mug wall. I thought it would be fun to let my regular customers keep their favorite mug here." She picked up the label gun and pointed it at him. "They can label their spot, so no one uses their cups."

"Sounds unsanitary."

Lauren gave an exasperated sigh and shook her head. "Whatever. How about you help me? I have a bunch of mismatched mugs that I'm going to hang for anyone who doesn't have their own." She motioned to him. "Follow me."

Paul followed Lauren like her pup around the display counter and through the door leading into the kitchen. He gave a low whistle when he saw the gleaming stainless-steel island in the middle of the room. Everything was spotless. Industrial-size blenders and several appliances he couldn't identify lined the counter perpendicular to the huge double sink.

"This is where the magic happens," he said with an appreciative nod.

"This is it. My happy place." Lauren's face fell. "Until today, that is."

Paul feigned ignorance. "Why? What happened?"

Lauren reached into a cupboard and pulled out several mismatched cups and mugs. "Ugh. My identity was stolen." She turned to face him with a scowl. "If I could find who did that, I'd … well, it wouldn't be pretty."

"I believe you." Paul helped carry several mugs back into the dining area. "What are you going to do?"

Lauren's face was taut. "I'm not sure. The bank is supposed to be able to get my money back. But there's still the issue of my credit."

Paul handed the mugs to Lauren one at a time. She hung them on random wood pegs.

"I have to contact all three reporting agencies and freeze my credit. And something has to be done about those new credit cards that are already maxed out."

Paul shoved his hands into his pockets. "Perhaps I can help."

Lauren's hands dropped to her sides. She gazed up at him with eyes filled with hope. "How?"

"I have a brilliant legal team. Would you let me contact them and see what they can do?"

Lauren frowned. "I don't have any money to pay an attorney."

"You wouldn't have to. I keep them on retainer. It won't cost you anything."

Lauren's gaze dropped to the floor. "What about you? What do you get out of it?"

There had to be a quid pro quo. Nobody offered the services of their legal team for free. Probably a very expensive legal team.

"Thank you, anyway, but I'll figure it out." Lauren closed the door behind Paul and locked it.

"At least let me contact them for you. Get some advice?"

Lauren blew out a breath. "Fine." She grabbed a business card from the plastic holder next to the register. "Here." She handed the card to Paul.

He examined it for a moment. "Is this your business phone number?"

"Yes. Why?"

"Can you write your cell on the back? Might be easier to reach you."

He smiled that killer smile, revealing the dimple in one cheek.

"Very smooth, Mr. Montrose."

"Excuse me?"

"Smooth way to get my phone number." She made air quotes and said, "For my attorney."

Paul's grin returned. "What can I say? Smooth is my middle name."

Lauren shook her head. "Let's go back to the kitchen." She pulled two aprons off the wall hooks and tossed one in his direction. "Ever heard of rage baking?"

"Is that like stress eating?" Paul asked.

"Similar. You'd better shed that jacket. And roll up your sleeves too." Lauren took his suit coat and hung it on one of the apron hooks. "I'm going to let Molly out for a minute before I take her upstairs. Do you think you can figure out how to turn on that oven?" She pointed toward one of the over-sized ovens across the room.

"Sure," Paul said, slipping the apron over his head.

Lauren pulled a binder from one of the shelves and opened it. "Here's what we're going to be making," she said, pointing at a plastic-enclosed recipe. "Grab the eggs and milk from the fridge. I should be back in about ten minutes."

Paul fumbled with the apron ties. She spun him around by the shoulders and quickly tied the sash behind him. When she finished, Paul turned around to face her. They were inches apart.

"Perfect," Lauren said.

Paul's gaze pinned hers. "Yes. Perfect."

Lauren took a step back. "Okay. Well. Come on, Molly. Let's go outside."

She resisted the urge to fan herself with one hand while leading her pup out the door.

Touching Paul had been a bad idea. His well-muscled shoulders were warm under her hands. The white dress shirt fit him like it was custom-made. And it probably was. No doubt about it, the man was attractive. Could it be his attraction to her was not simply about getting into her pants?

Mom's voice crashed against Samantha's.

No man wants a fat girl.

You are fun, funny, and an amazing cook.

Paul could have any woman he wanted. Why her?

As if conjured up by some cosmic force, Sam sent a text.

Can you talk?

Lauren dialed her sister's number while Molly sniffed the bushes along the fence.

"What's up, Sam?"

"My photo shoot in Florida was cancelled."

"I'm sorry to hear that. Why?"

"There's the threat of a hurricane. I was thinking I'd come up and stay with you for a couple of days."

"And sleep on my sofa bed? You hate that."

Sam's sigh blew through the phone. "I know. But I want to meet this billionaire of yours. You know, give him the sniff test. Make sure he isn't going to hurt you."

Lauren shook her head. "Paul is not my billionaire. We've gone out one time." Lauren didn't mention that Paul was currently in her kitchen.

"Yeah, but I'm bored. Please let me come. I'll help in your shop."

"Of course. And bring a pile of money with you." Lauren explained what happened with her bank account and credit cards.

Sam was suitably shocked and angry. "Holy cats, Lauren. That's terrible. Let me help."

"Fine, but it will be a loan, okay?"

"Sure. I'll be there Friday afternoon."

They disconnected and Lauren guided Molly up the outside stairs and into the apartment. She put her puppy into the kennel and returned downstairs.

Paul sat on one of the stools at the center island, thumbing through his phone. He looked up when she entered. "That was longer than ten minutes."

"My sister called. She's coming to visit this weekend."

"Brilliant. Why don't you and she come with me to check on the house I'm remodeling on Lake Keuka?"

Lauren was already shaking her head before Paul finished his sentence. No way would she let him meet her super-model sister. One look at Sam and he'd never even glance her direction again.

"I don't think that's a good idea," Lauren said, tightening her apron strings.

"I think it's a brilliant idea. Didn't you tell me your sister is a model?"

Lauren narrowed her eyes. "Yes …"

Paul turned his phone around, so the screen faced her. On it was a photo of Samantha posing in a couture gown. "Is this her?"

Lauren's stomach dropped. Whatever attraction may have been growing between her and Paul, it was now over. "Yeah, that's my sister."

"I knew it! I'd love to meet her. We were at the same fundraiser last year. There was a fashion show auction-type thing, and your sister was one of the models."

Lauren turned toward the cupboard where she kept the flour and sugar. "Awesome," she said without enthusiasm.

Paul's voice was close behind when he spoke. "I can see the resemblance."

Lauren whirled around, their faces inches apart. "I look nothing like Sam," she said in a breathless whisper.

Paul touched her nose with his index finger. "I see the resemblance here." He tapped her cheek. "And here." Her chin. "And here." He rested his finger on her lips. "Here."

Her breath caught as she stared into his ice-blue eyes. Holy cow was he going to kiss her? A nervous giggle worked its way up from her belly, followed by sheer terror. After the disastrous way her ex had departed, her self-esteem still suffered. She'd never be good enough.

# Chapter 17

The kitchen was heating up and not merely from the oven. He should never have touched her. Lauren's skin was warm and soft as a ripe peach. With her back pressed up against the counter, he could have kissed her. But the flash of fear in her eyes warned him not to try.

Paul dropped his hand and stepped back. "Tell me about this rage baking thing."

Lauren scrubbed her cheeks with her palms. Hopefully not to remove the feel of his finger.

She sucked in breath and blew it out. "Yes. Right. Baking." She pulled the three-ring binder toward her. "I have a contract to supply cupcakes for a friend's wedding."

"Cupcakes? I thought all you made were muffins."

Lauren sent him a sly glance. "Surely a Forbes guy would know it's important to diversify."

Paul threw back his head and laughed. "Of course."

Lauren leaned over the recipe book. "My friend has Celiac so she asked if I can make red velvet cupcakes gluten free. I think I've got it down after several disasters." She looked up to catch his eye. "Want to help?"

Paul's heart thumped against his ribcage. "Yes."

Lauren cleared her throat. "Okay. First, I have to thoroughly wash anything that might have come in contact with non-gluten-free flour."

Paul spent the next twenty minutes with his hands thrust into hot soapy water. Once he'd washed and dried bowls, spoons, and various mixer implements, Lauren was ready to begin assembling the batter.

"This is a lot of work," Paul commented when they'd filled the muffin tins and shoved them into the oven. "You do this every day?"

"Every day except Sunday and Monday."

"Why do you call it rage baking?"

Lauren huffed out a laugh. "If I've had a particularly stressful day, I start throwing things together and try to come up with new recipe ideas. It helps relieve the stress." She shrugged. "Sounds silly."

"Not at all. When I'm stressed, I cook. Usually something involving red meat."

Lauren sent him a skeptical look. "Really?"

"Really. And then I eat it. Hence my weight challenges."

"You? Have weight challenges? Hah."

Paul hesitated before answering. He still pictured himself as a chubby man, even after losing six stones. Or ninety pounds. Why would a woman as beautiful and accomplished as Lauren be interested in him?

Paul focused his gaze on the flour dusting the island surface. "After my parents died, I ate my way through grief. Do you have any idea how easy it is to pack on weight and how difficult it is to shed?"

Lauren made a derisive sound. "You're kidding, right?" She slapped her hands against her stomach.

"See this? It's called 'let's sample one of everything in the display case.' Remember that rage baking thing? It's usually followed by rage eating."

Could it be they had something in common? It would seem so. Paul inhaled and decided to leap into unfamiliar territory—vulnerability.

"I, uh, still feel chuffed no matter how much weight I lose."

"Chuffed?"

"Fat. Bloated. Chubby. Puffed up—"

"Got it."

Paul felt Lauren's eyes on him. Was she judging or sympathetic. He dared himself to raise his head. She studied him for several tense moments.

"I believe you," she said.

Paul shot to his feet and reached behind him to untie his apron. Slipping it over his head, he tossed it on the stool he'd vacated. "I should go."

He pulled his suit coat from the peg and slung it over one shoulder.

"Wait," Lauren said, getting to her feet.

Paul waited.

She seemed to come to a decision with a nod of her head. "I'd love to go with you to see your remodel."

Paul's face stretched into a grin. "Splendid. And we'll let your sister tag along, will we?"

Lauren pressed her lips together, then said, "Sure."

Paul let himself out of the Muffin Top and whistled as he sauntered down the street. Until he remembered he'd have to walk back to the Air B&B unless he called Marvin.

Nope, the walk would do him good. And give him a chance to rehash every bit of his time with Lauren.

Lauren wiped her forehead with the back of one hand. With the other she opened the oven door to check the doneness of the cupcakes.

"Perfect," she said aloud, pulling the first tray from the oven. She placed both trays on cooling racks.

After washing one of the mixing bowls, she started preparing the frosting. Marnie had been specific on the type of whipped frosting she wanted for the wedding cupcakes. Lauren was happy to oblige.

Lauren returned upstairs to her apartment while the cupcakes cooled. She let Molly out and they clomped down the stairs to the backyard.

"Well, Molly girl, what do you think about that?" Molly looked at her as if to say I have no idea what you're talking about.

Lauren tossed a ball for Molly to chase and thought back over every moment of her time with Paul. She cringed, remembering how she'd blasted him when he asked about hugging Mike. She'd held her breath when he touched her face, wondering—hoping—he might kiss her.

But fear of rejection had made her hesitate. Once Paul met Samantha, would he shift his attention to her?

And his confession about self-image. That was eye-opening. Could it be he didn't care that she carried extra pounds? Sam insisted her curves made her look like one of those Greek statues of voluptuous women.

"I'm jealous you can eat whatever and whenever you want," Sam had said. "I have to limit my calorie intake to a thousand. Per day. Forget eating even three crumbs of one of your fabulous muffins."

"Sucks to be you," Lauren had shot back.

When Molly dropped to her tummy at Lauren's feet, sides heaving, she knew it was time to return the pup to her bed.

Meanwhile, Lauren set to work on removing the cupcakes from the baking tins. She slathered icing on one and took a huge bite.

"Perfect." She'd offer them to the regular group of men she called the One Syllables. If Jim, Tom, Tim, Bob, and Steve liked them, they'd be good enough to serve at Marnie's wedding.

Later as she prepared for bed, her cell rang with an unfamiliar number. Normally she didn't answer unrecognized numbers.

"Hello?"

A familiar voice came through the phone. "Oh, hello. I was checking to be sure I had your number correct. You know, for the attorney."

Lauren grinned into the phone. Paul, the billionaire Forbes cover guy, sounded nervous.

"Who is this?"

"This is Paul. Montrose."

"Paul? Do I know you?"

There was a moment of silence before he responded. Lauren heard the smile in his voice. "You might recognize me from the recent Forbes Magazine write up."

"Oh, that Paul Montrose."

"Very funny."

"You have the number correct, Mr. Montrose. Or may I call you Paul?"

"Please do. How did the red cupcakes turn out?"

"Yummy. I'll save you one."

"Promise?"

"Absolutely. Now let me go. I have my alarm set for four-thirty a.m."

"Ouch. Very well. Good night, Lauren."

"Goodnight, Paul."

Lauren hugged the phone to her chest and squealed.

# Chapter 18

**Paul arrived at** the bank early and turned off the alarm. He set the 'all clear' signal and sat in his office. He'd have to hustle to get caught up on emails and other administrative tasks before the tee time with the guys. He quashed the momentary irritation with Ian from the day before. His ability to compartmentalize helped him focus on what needed to be done today.

Carol had Bcc'd him on the email sent to the board asking for their approval to close down the SBA loan department. Except for one board member, Martha Livingston, all had agreed to the wisdom of cutting the cost of required maintenance and reporting to the Federal Small Business Administration.

With a satisfied sigh, he drafted a letter to be sent to all SBA loan holders giving them sixty days to find other financing before their loans were called.

Soon he'd have the bank on good financial footing, and he could move on to the next challenge.

A vision of Lauren caught him off guard. Was she more than a new challenge? His MO was discover, conquer, move on. What was it about the woman that captivated his mind. And possibly his heart.

It was too soon to go that far. Why was he so

anxious to show her his new home on Lake Keuka? It was the sort of place he could see himself settling down in. But his nature was not to settle down. After Lauren, would he want to see what other areas needed to be conquered?

Time to go back to work. Thinking about Lauren was a distraction he didn't need right now. Paul reworded the letter and sent it to Carol, asking her to print it on bank letterhead and leave it on his desk.

As he stood and stretched, Carol herself unlocked the front door and stepped into the lobby. "I didn't expect to see you here so early," she said, dropping her purse and lunch bag on her desk.

"I came in early to get some work done. I have a golf game schedule with John Druban at ten."

Carol nodded and turned the 'all clear' sign around.

"I sent you a couple of emails," Paul said before Carol crossed the lobby. "Thank you for acting as my de facto administrative assistant."

"No problem."

Paul watched her back as she headed toward the break room, presumably to store her lunch in the refrigerator. He'd have to find a way to make up for his harshness the day before. In the meantime, he'd head to the Muffin Top and see if Lauren had, indeed, saved him one of those red cupcakes. He'd make up for the calories by walking part of the golf course instead of using the cart.

Sure, justify it, Mate.

All right, conscience. Time to shut it.

"Carol, as soon as Margie gets here, I'm heading out to grab a coffee. Want anything?"

Carol crossed the lobby and sat at her desk. "Where

are you going?"

Paul felt his face warm. "The Muffin Top."

"You could bring me back one of their blueberry muffins. Or whatever the flavor of the day is. I'm not picky."

"Very well. Consider it done."

Paul returned to his office and donned his suit jacket as Margie came through the front door.

"Want a muffin?" Paul asked.

"Ooh, sure. Anything is fine."

With a wave to his employees, Paul set off toward Lauren's bakery. He'd buy a dozen and take them back for the rest of the staff. And why not? He was all about supporting small business. The fact that his new favorite person owned the business was a plus.

Paul opened the door to the Muffin Top and was assaulted by the smell of sugar and spice. He inhaled and was escorted back in time to his mother's kitchen. As a small boy, he'd loved to help her cook. His friends chided him for being a sissy, but Paul didn't care. Dad never degraded his love for cooking.

Paul watched Lauren chat with a table of gray-haired men. Must be the 'one syllables' she'd mentioned. The look in the men's eyes as they talked with her were a sight to behold. Each had a cupcake in front of them in various degrees of consumption. From what he could hear, they each had an opinion. But most were positive. Would they discover the treat was gluten free? Sometimes hearing the words meant 'flavor free' as well. Paul couldn't wait to taste one.

As if feeling his presence, Lauren turned and sent a brilliant smile in his direction. His heart sped up and his stomach flip flopped. He was smitten.

Lauren turned to see Paul standing in the door of her bakery. The conversation around her seemed to lower in volume and every thought fled. Paul's smile warmed her from the top of her head to her tip toes.

She was caught in a snare she had no desire to escape from. The way he looked at her made her feel like she was the only person in the room. A cough from one of the One Syllables snapped her back. Lauren half-turned to find eight sets of eyes staring at her with one singular look. Amusement.

"Better go wait on your customer," Jim said with a smirk.

"Don't want to keep Mr. Suit waiting," Bob chimed in.

The others made similar comments while Lauren fought to keep herself from blushing.

She gripped the front of her apron and walked behind the display case as Paul approached.

"Hi," he said.

"Hi," Lauren echoed.

They stared at each other until the bell jingled over the door, signaling another customer.

Paul cleared his throat. "I'd, uh, like a dozen muffins. Assorted."

"Of course." Lauren reached behind her for a box. "I'll be with you in a moment," she said to the two ladies who'd come in behind Paul.

Paul's voice was low as he said, "Did you save me a cupcake?"

Lauren blinked. "Yes."

When she'd packed the muffins into the box, Paul pulled out a hundred-dollar bill. Lauren rang up his purchase, noting again how he put the change in the tip jar. Kennedy would go home happy again today.

"I'll get your cupcake after I help these ladies."

Paul nodded and stepped aside.

Lauren's impatience rose as the two older women debated over their choice of muffin.

"I think maybe the pumpkin one. Or no, maybe the oat bran." She looked at Lauren with watery blue eyes. "Which is healthier? My doctor said I have to cut down."

Lauren sucked in a breath, resisting the urge to say, 'I don't know!'

"Why don't you get the one you want today? You can always cut down tomorrow."

This brought a giggle from the two women. Lauren glanced at Paul with a 'what can you do?' eye roll.

When they'd paid for their choices and searched for a mug on her new pegboard, she raised her index finger signaling him to wait while she went into the kitchen.

"What's got you all smiley?" Kennedy asked, pulling a fresh muffin tray from the oven.

"Nothing." Lauren avoided Kennedy's gaze while she carefully packed the red velvet cupcake in a small to-go box.

"It's him, isn't it? Mr. South Africa."

"Maybe."

"I knew it. You're crushing on him, aren't you?"

"No."

"Liar. Say, did he bring his assistant in? The cute Black guy? What was his name?"

"Marvin," Lauren said, then regretted being so

quick to answer.

"You've been awfully tight-lipped about your date on Sunday."

"I've had a lot on my mind," Lauren said, reminding Kennedy of the identity theft.

Kennedy sent her a knowing look. "Fine, but when you get this mess straightened out, I want deets."

Lauren huffed. "It's going to take weeks to get it straightened out. I'm going to have to get an attorney involved." She placed the box into a carry bag and headed toward the door to the dining area.

"Sounds expensive," Kennedy commented.

Lauren shrugged, unwilling to mention Paul's offer of representation by his firm.

She returned to the front and found Paul chatting with the One Syllables.

"Here you go," she said, handing Paul the small carry bag.

"Special treatment, eh?" Bob asked.

"No more special than you reprobates," Lauren said, using one hand to shove Paul toward the door. She ignored the sly comments from her regulars.

Before they reached the door, Bob called out, "Way to go, mate!"

Lauren turned to find Bob holding his hand in a thumbs up gesture. She shook her head with a smile. Those guys were like having six dads.

She escorted Paul out the door and stood with her arms crossed. "Sorry about that."

"No worries. They obviously care about you. With good reason."

"Sometimes I think it's just because I feed them."

"You know what they say about the way to a man's

heart."

Was that the way to Paul's heart? Was his interest in her more than someone who filled a need for the moment? He had the ability to buy anything he wanted. Was he trying to buy her affection, or was his interest real?

Lauren had determined after the guy whose name isn't uttered she wouldn't settle for anything less than a man's whole heart.

# Chapter 19

The rest of Lauren's week sped by. Kennedy offered to close on Saturday so Lauren could spend time with her sister. Samantha arrived Friday afternoon in a cloud of expensive perfume.

"Lauren!" Sam wheeled her suitcase through the bakery door and spread her arms. "Come give your sister a hug."

Every head swiveled to stare at Lauren's sister. From the top of her blonde highlights to the tips of the Louboutin shoes, Samantha was a walking couture ad. Pink slacks hugged Sam's hips down to her ankles. The pink, black, and gray plaid jacket hit at Sam's narrow waist.

Lauren imagined everyone's gaze traveling from Sam to her and back. Talk about the ugly duckling and the swan.

"Look at you," Lauren said as Sam pulled her in for a hug. "Perfect as usual." Her voice held no rancor. She loved her sister to death and didn't envy Sam's lifestyle. She'd have hives if she had to prance in front of judgmental fashion critics.

"Look at you," Sam said, holding Lauren by the shoulders. "You look different." She made a show of turning Lauren left and right. She leaned in and whispered, "You have the look of a woman in love."

"Sam!"

Samantha laughed. "Just kidding. But I do want every single little detail."

Lauren shook her head with a wry grin. "Go take your stuff upstairs. Then come back down when you're wearing something you can get batter on."

When Samantha returned to the kitchen, she embraced Kennedy. "Thanks for putting up with my sister," she said. "What's she like as a boss?" Sam stuck a finger into a bowl of muffin batter.

Lauren smacked her shoulder. "Stop. Kennedy knows I'm the best boss in the world."

Kennedy smirked and pointed to Lauren. "We'll talk when she's not around."

"I love the mug board. That's new, right?"

Lauren smiled. "Mike did it."

"Ah, good old Mike." Sam turned to Kennedy. "Did Lauren tell you we all grew up together? Everyone wanted Mike and Lauren to get together, but I think he's still pining for me." She swept a dramatic hand across her forehead.

"You wish," Lauren retorted. "I think he has a girlfriend."

"Tell me it isn't so. My heart is broken." Sam sank onto a stool and leaned her arms on the counter.

Lauren handed her sister an apron. "So far, people seem to love the mug board. Did you notice some of the regulars have already claimed their spot."

"How'd they do that?" Samantha asked.

"I bought a label gun and left it on the counter. Everyone can label their mug and their place on the board. I saw it on Pinterest."

"Smart. Now, let's talk about Paul."

Lauren rolled her eyes. "Let's not."

"Have you talked to him today?"

Lauren focused on scraping the sides of a mixing bowl to get the last of the batter into a waiting muffin tin. "We've been so busy I've barely had time to say hello when he comes in for his morning fix."

"What about texts?"

Lauren kept her face averted. There'd been a few texts between her and Paul. Mostly low-level flirting.

Thinking about you.

Thanks for the muffin.

How's your day going?

Your attorney contacted me.

Can't wait for Saturday.

"A few," Lauren said. She looked up to see Sam watching her with pursed lips.

Sam raised her eyebrows. "What should I expect tomorrow? What time are we leaving to check out this guy's mansion?"

"Who said it was a mansion?"

"Rich guy. House on Keuka Lake. Remodel. That's how you spell mansion."

"Whatever. He's going to pick us up around noon. Kennedy graciously offered to close up for me. And to take Molly home."

Sam shifted her gaze to Kennedy. "I'm thinking that any man who wants to show a woman his home is a man who is looking for a relationship. Do you agree?"

Kennedy's head bobbed up and down. "I'd say so. You should see the way he looks at her when he comes in. Like she's one of the muffins and he'd like to gobble her up."

Lauren raised her palms to her cheeks. "Stop it you two. Paul has never given any indication he wants to pursue a relationship. We've had one date. One date."

Sam and Kennedy exchanged a glance. "Uh huh," they said at the same time.

Paul woke Saturday morning and stretched his arms over his head. Today would be a great day after a great week. The board had unanimously agreed with his reorganization plans for the bank. Even Martha Livingston had come around. Letters had gone out to all the SBA loan holders. He'd soon hire a bank manager and leave the institution in that man or woman's capable hands.

But today he'd forget business and spend the afternoon with Lauren and her sister. Marvin had made sure the lake house was clean after the construction crew finished. He'd also arranged for food to be delivered there. Paul planned to serve a late lunch for the women and spend time on the massive deck overlooking the lake.

Paul padded to the kitchen and filled the electric kettle with water. While it heated, he mentally reviewed his agenda for the day.

Review the counteroffer from the owner of the Air B&B where he and Marvin were currently staying. Ask Marvin to contact the movers to clear their things out of the rental.

He paused. Would Marvin prefer to stay here in Hornell rather than move to Keuka Lake? The new house was big enough to house several families but perhaps Marvin would appreciate having privacy. Would the logistics work if they lived in two different places?

Paul admitted he'd been spoiled by having Marvin so close. In The City, Marvin had his own apartment, albeit in the same building as Paul. But with them both staying in the rental, Paul could speak to him directly at a moment's notice.

Yes, perhaps Marvin would rather have some personal space. He'd bring the subject up on the way to pick up Lauren and her sister.

His nerves danced at the thought of spending over an hour in the back seat of the Escalade with Lauren. Should he buy flowers? No, he'd look like a spanner if he didn't do the same for Samantha. Ugh. So awkward.

Paul dressed in a pair of light slacks and a teal golf shirt, reminding himself to bring a pair of shorts in case it was hot on the lake. He glanced out the window as he slid his feet into a pair of Hey Dudes.

A few bruise-like clouds skittered across the sky. No rain today, please, he implored the heavens.

When he returned to the kitchen, the electric kettle had switched off, but the water still bubbled. Carrying a cup of his special Bewley's Tea, he padded to the deck. The wind kicked up loose leaves and sent them twirling. Even if the weather turned nasty, the day promised to be a good one.

The house on Keuka Lake turned out better than he'd expected. He rubbed his hands together anticipating the move. Being on the water had a calming effect. He pictured long lazy summer days relaxing on the dock in a lounge chair. Perhaps he'd buy a boat and drop the anchor somewhere in the middle of the lake.

Reality smacked him back to the present. He'd never been one to sit still for long. He'd be bored within a day. Unless—the thought took hold—he had someone to spend the idle time with.

Being single was lame. Single and wealthy took lame to another level. Women on the prowl for a sugar sponsor were like hungry piranhas sensing a drop of blood. He'd even had sixty-year-old plus women attach themselves to his side at various fund-raisers. He shuddered, remembering their talon-like clutches on his arm.

Thank the good Lord Lauren seemed unmoved by his money. He did notice her raised eyebrows at the change he jammed into the tip jar after each purchase. Knowing her, she'd passed that money on to her employee.

The woman was amazing. Angry and ready to cry one moment and helping him tie on an apron the next.

Today should prove interesting.

# Chapter 20

**Samantha's voice echoed** up the stairs as Lauren changed clothes for the third time. "Hurry up."

When did dressing for an outing become such a big deal?

"It is when you're going on an outing with a billionaire," Lauren said to Molly. Her pup yipped in agreement. She cupped her hands around her mouth and shouted, "I'll be right down."

Finally settling on a pair of loose palazzo pants and a white tee, Lauren grabbed a sweater and clomped down the stairs, followed by her puppy.

"Ken, will you please take Molly upstairs after I leave? I'm going to let her out to do her business."

Kendall nodded her agreement. "You got it. Oh, the mail came while you were getting dressed." Kendall shoved a stack of letters in Lauren's direction.

Lauren took the mail without looking at it and stuck it in her carry bag along with the sweater.

Sam tapped her foot. "I thought I took a long time to get ready."

Lauren shrugged. "I have doubts about today."

Sam linked her arm with Lauren's and pulled her

out the door. "It'll be fun."

Paul leaned against the side of the SUV staring down at his phone as Lauren and Sam approached. He straightened and shoved his phone into his pocket. His gaze traveled from Lauren's head down to her feet. She held her breath when he approached.

Holding out his hand, he said, "You must be Lauren's sister. I'm pleased to meet you."

As soon as they'd shaken hands, Paul turned his back to Samantha and took Lauren's arm. "You look beautiful," he said.

Emotion swelled in her throat, choking off her ability to answer. Paul's response was different from every other man she'd introduced to her sister. Their look of disbelief that they were related was usually followed by rapt adoration of Sam's beauty. Paul seemed not to care.

Marvin opened the passenger door of the Escalade. "Sir, will you be sitting up front?"

"Let's let Samantha sit up front. I'll take the back with Lauren."

Sam sent Lauren a smirk.

"Very good." Marvin waited for Sam to climb in.

Once they were buckled in, Marvin said, "It's about an hour drive to the lake. Does anyone need to stop anywhere along the way?"

Lauren chuckled. "Have you driven to Keuka Lake? There aren't a lot of places to stop."

Paul's smile was warm when he turned in her direction. "It's a beautiful drive."

"Looks like we might get some rain," Marvin commented, pointing out the windshield.

"Even so, it is still a beautiful drive."

Lauren searched her brain for something to start a conversation. Finally, she said, "How was your week?"

"Fruitful," Paul replied. "How was yours?"

"Busy. Thank you again for referring me to your attorney. She is helping me wade through all the paperwork I need to fight this identity theft."

"My pleasure. Did the bank refund your money?"

Paul wracked his brain trying to remember if he'd told Lauren he owned the bank. He'd meant to check her account to ensure her funds had been recovered, but since Tuesday, he'd been swamped with work.

"Yes, Carol at the bank told me twenty-four to forty-eight hours. It's called a provisional credit, though. I guess the fraud department has to make sure the money really is mine."

Paul noted the furrow between her brows. "I'm sure it will all work out."

"I hope so."

The last thing he wanted was for Lauren's money woes to keep her from having a good day. Time to distract.

"Did you know Keuka Lake is Y-shaped, unlike the other Finger Lakes? Keuka means 'lake with an elbow' in the Seneca language."

Lauren turned an amused glanced toward him. "No kidding."

Paul felt his face grow hot. Lauren must think he was nit. He sucked in a breath and blew it out. "My house is near the town of Hammondsport in Pulteney. It doesn't look like much from the road, but it's right on the lake. Next summer I'm thinking about buying a boat. The water looks brilliant."

"What have you done to the house?"

Paul rubbed a hand through his hair. "The roof needed to be replaced. I also had the kitchen gutted. The cabinets were the same wood as the wood floors and plank ceiling." Paul gave a mock shudder. "All that wood. I had it painted, of course. Some previous owner thought every bedroom and bath should be light blue."

The side of Lauren's mouth tilted up. "Oh, the horrors."

"Once I get settled in, I'll remodel the basement. There's a full kitchen down there and a couple of bedrooms. The think I'm most excited about is it's right on the lakefront."

"It sounds awesome."

Paul stared down at Lauren's hand resting on the space between them. What would it be like to live in his beautiful new home completely alone? Ghastly. At thirty-four, he was tired of living by himself. These past couple of months at the Air B&B in Hornell with Marvin had spoiled him. He liked knowing someone else was in the house.

He'd amassed enough wealth to keep him comfortably the rest of his life. But it was a lonely life. Paul longed for someone to share it with.

He laid a hand on top of Lauren's and gently squeezed it. She swiveled her head toward him and regarded him with wide hazel eyes. His heart did a flip flop. He was taken in by this woman.

The moment was broken when Lauren's sister twisted in her seat and said, "What part of South Africa are you from?"

Paul left his hand on Lauren's, hoping her sister wouldn't notice. He cleared his throat. "Durbin. How did you know I'm from South Africa? Most people think I have a British accent."

"Lauren had a boyfriend from there. I recognized your accent right away."

Paul sent a questioning look toward Lauren, but she'd turned to stare out the window. What an odd coincidence she had an ex from his country.

The wind picked up outside the vehicle, tossing leaves against the windshield. A bit of rain pattered on the road, obscuring the view.

"Looks like that storm is going to hit us head on," Marvin said, knuckles white on the steering wheel.

Paul released Lauren's hand and leaned forward. "It's only a few more miles, isn't it?"

"Yup." Marvin slowed the SUV as they entered the village of Hammondsport. The road wound through houses, restaurants, and shops before opening up to a view of Keuka Lake.

"There it is," Sam said from the front seat. "It's beautiful, even with the rain coming down."

Marvin pulled close to the house and put the car in park. "I have the keys. Let me open up before you make a dash through the rain." He pulled on a baseball cap and ran around the car to the one door visible from the road.

When Marvin had unlocked the door, Paul jumped out and helped Lauren open her car door. Marvin returned to help Sam out.

"Go on inside," Paul instructed.

They trooped into the house and closed the door against the storm.

Paul felt a jolt of satisfaction at Lauren's gasp.
"Beautiful," she breathed.

# Chapter 21

The matching red leather sofas on either side of the stone fireplace called Lauren to sink into their plushness. She saw herself kicking off her shoes and letting her toes sink into the red, black, and gray area rug between the sofas.

She walked to the windows overlooking the deck. Although the rain tapped against the glass, the lake was visible down below the house.

"Want the fifty-cent tour?" Paul asked, joining her at the window.

"Sure."

Sam hung her purse on a coat rack inside the front door. "I'll help Marvin set out lunch," she said. She sent Lauren a knowing look.

Paul guided Lauren through the upstairs. Lauren noted how he glowed with pride over the way the remodel had turned out. Vaulted ceilings gave the impression of space, and almost all the windows faced the lake.

"Do you want to see the basement?" Paul asked, pointing down the stairs. "It hasn't been touched yet, but maybe you can give me some suggestions."

Lauren preceded him down the stairs to a massive

room complete with a full-sized ping pong table.

"I love ping pong," Lauren said, running her hand along the white stripe at the edge of the table.

"I'll have to order a set of paddles," Paul said. "I haven't played since college. I'm a pretty good table tennis player, if I do say so myself."

Lauren smiled. "Challenge accepted."

She loved the way Paul's eyes crinkled at the edges when he smiled. He should smile more often. She should get him to smile more often.

Where did that thought come from?

Paul showed her every bedroom in the basement, including a bath and a half. "I can't believe there's another kitchen down here," he said, shaking his head. It's like a completely different house."

Lauren gazed out the window at the boat dock, bobbing in the lake's whitecaps. "It's so close to the water. You could get up in the morning and walk out and have your coffee—wait, is that a bar out there?"

Paul joined her, his shoulder touching hers as they peered out the window.

"Yes, it is. Not stocked right now, of course. But, yes, it's a bar with a couple of stools."

Lauren's excitement grew as she thought about how awesome it would be to live in a place like this. "You could have your morning coffee out there and stare at the water. That would be a great way to start the day."

Paul murmured his agreement.

"This house was made for entertaining. I'm sure you know that. Think about how you could invite all your friends to stay. There are so many places to sleep down here. Like a huge slumber party."

"Or room for a growing family." Paul's words hung

in the air.

Lauren swallowed against the sudden lump her throat. "Do you want kids?" Her voice came out in a whisper.

"Yes. I do."

Lauren braved a glance at him, only to find he'd turned and was staring down at her.

"Oh," she said.

Paul leaned forward a few inches until their faces were close. "When I find the right woman."

Lauren's breath hitched. Was he going to kiss her? Did she want him to?

Yes, she did. What would his lips feel like? Warm and inviting like the sofas upstairs? Or cold and calculating like the businessman he was?

Lauren moved her head slightly toward him. Paul lowered his head and gently placed his lips on hers. Heat exploded from her chest, warming her core. This first kiss was everything a first kiss should be. Tender, tentative, and totally captivating.

Paul circled his arms around her and pulled her closer. Her eyes fluttered open to find his gaze staring at her like she was the most beautiful woman in the world. At that moment, Lauren felt that way.

She wrapped her arms around him, pulled him close, and laid a palm on his strong jaw. Standing on tip toes, she pulled his head down for a second kiss.

"Hey, guys, lunch is ready." Sam's voice echoed from the top of the stairs.

Lauren jerked as Paul dropped his arms to his sides. A giggle rose from her tummy and escaped.

Paul cleared his throat. "I guess we'd better go upstairs." He ran a hand across his face with a rueful grin.

"Yeah, we'd better."

Lauren blew out a breath as she climbed the stairs. Was their kiss evident on her face? If so, she'd have some explaining to do to her sister.

The storm had increased in intensity and rain battered the windows. Angry waves crashed onto the shore, washing over the boat dock.

"I'm glad we're inside," Lauren said.

"Indeed." Paul motioned for her to take a seat at the table.

"This looks delicious, Marvin," Lauren said, sitting next to her sister.

"I couldn't have done it without Miss Samantha's help," Marvin said.

Marvin had laid out a feast of various kinds of lunchmeat, cheese, and an assortment of sandwich rolls. Another platter had pickles, olives, and cut up veggies.

"Does anyone want some soup?" Marvin asked, hovering near the stove.

"Sure," Sam said. "I'll have to fast for the next week after today. But it will be worth it."

While Marvin dished up bowls of steaming clam chowder, Paul peppered Sam with questions.

"I remember seeing you at a fashion show in New York City. Do you often do charitable events like that one?"

"On occasion. When my agent thinks it'll be good for my career."

"How did you get started modeling?"

Sam rolled her eyes. "It's a long story. And boring. I'll have Lauren tell you someday."

Lauren wanted to bless her sister. She'd turned the

attention from herself back to Lauren.

Sam took a spoonful of soup, swallowed it, and groaned. "This is delicious."

Marvin grinned. "One of my many talents."

"Lauren is a great cook, too," Sam said.

"I thought all she knew how to make was muffins," Paul said with a teasing tone.

"Let's not forget cupcakes," Lauren said, shaking a finger at him.

Sam pointed her spoon in Paul's direction. "Don't let her fool you. She's not just another pretty face. She can cook up a storm when she wants to."

Paul's look in Lauren's direction smoldered. "You'll have to show me sometime."

Lauren dropped her gaze to her plate. Now she wished Sam would stop. This was getting embarrassing.

"So, Paul, what exactly do you do?" Sam asked.

"Mostly real estate investing. Although lately I've taken on a troubled business and am in the process of turning it around."

"Sounds interesting. What kind of business?"

Paul glanced at Lauren before he opened his mouth.

Everyone jumped when a crash sounded from outside.

"What was that?" Paul exclaimed, jumping up from his chair.

Marvin rushed to the door and peered outside. "Bad news, Mr. Montrose."

Paul joined him at the window. He pulled the door open to reveal a massive tree had fallen on the roof of the Escalade. He pushed the door closed as rain pelted him.

"That is not good." Paul chewed his lip and brushed water from his shoulders. He turned toward the ladies. "We may be stuck here for a bit."

"What was that?" Lauren asked as she and Sam slid their chairs back to join them.

Paul moved aside and pointed out the window. "That happened."

"Oh no!"

"I'll make some calls," Marvin said. "You guys go back to the table and finish eating."

Paul sent him a grateful smile. Marvin would take care of things like he always did.

"Marvin is right. Let's enjoy this meal while we wait for a car."

They finished eating in silence. Marvin had retreated to the basement to use his cell.

"I'll clean up," Samantha said when they were done.

"I'll help." Lauren rose and began to clear their plates.

Paul headed downstairs to see if Marvin had any luck arranging for a rental. Marvin held his phone in one hand with a disgusted look.

"What is it?" Paul asked.

"I can't get through to any of the tow services. Everyone is out helping people who've been in accidents due to the storm. Or so their voicemail suggests."

"What about Marta in our New York office?"

"It's Saturday, Sir. No one is in the office."

Paul's irritation rose. Why wasn't Marvin on this?

"Did you try her cell?"

"The cell towers are jammed right now. Apparently, this storm has affected cell service." He waved his phone like a magic wand. If only.

"There must be something you can do." Paul regretted his annoyed tone the minute the words left his lips.

Marvin's face tightened. "I'm not a miracle worker." He strode into one of the bedrooms and slammed the door.

Paul wanted to pound his fist on the door and insist Marvin figure something out. How dare he walk away. He paid Marvin a lot of money to make things easier for him.

Striding to the window, he shoved his hands in his pockets and stared out at the deluge. Raindrops hit the dock's wood planks and bounced up. Down here in the basement, no outside sound penetrated the thick walls and triple-paned windows. The only sound was his conscience telling him he'd behaved badly.

He'd inherited his quick temper from his Da. That and his stubbornness. Not a great combination for personal relationships.

Paul sank onto one of the chairs left behind by the previous owner and let his head drop. A verse from his childhood catechism classes pierced his heart.

"Be angry and do not sin."

Blast. Another apology was needed. But would Marvin forgive him yet again?

# Chapter 22

"What do you suppose they're doing down there?" Samantha asked pointing toward the stairs.

Lauren sat on one of the sofas facing the wall of windows and pulled her bag toward her. "I don't know but hopefully they're finding a ride for us. Otherwise, we're stuck here for a while."

"Might not be a bad thing," Sam said waggling her eyebrows.

Lauren pulled the letters from her bag and thumbed through them. "Bill, bill, and a letter from my bank. Maybe it's about my money."

She used a finger to tear open the envelope.

"Dear SBA Loan Customer,

Our records indicate you have a loan with First Upstate Bank through the Small Business Administration. This letter is to inform you we have decided to close our SBA department. You have sixty days from the date of this letter to find alternate financing.

We apologize for any inconvenience this may cause. If you have any questions, please do not hesitate to contact the bank at 971-xxx-xxxx.

Sincerely,

Paul Montrose
President and CEO"


The letter fell from Lauren's stiff fingers.

"What is it?" Sam asked. "Aren't they going to give you back your money?"

Lauren could barely swallow. "Worse."

Sam sank onto the sofa and shoved Lauren's bag to the floor. Grabbing the letter, she scanned it. "This is terrible. You'll have to get another loan."

Lauren's eyes filled with tears. "It's worse than that."

Sam's forehead crinkled. "How so?"

Lauren pointed at the paper on Sam's lap. "Look at the signature."

Sam gasped. "Maybe it's a coincidence."

Lauren sprang to her feet at strode to the window. She whirled to face her sister. "How did I not know Paul was the CEO of my bank? Why didn't he say something?"

Sam waved a hand. "Maybe he didn't know you had a loan there?"

"Oh, come on, Sam. Don't be stupid. He had to have known I'm a customer."

"Then get another loan."

Lauren pulled in a breath and blew it out. "Sure. Now that my credit is in the toilet, qualifying for another loan should be a piece of cake."

"Oh, I forgot about that." Sam's gaze traveled around the room. "I could lend you some money. I have a healthy savings account. How much would you need."

Lauren snorted. "Two hundred thirty thousand dollars."

Sam pinched her lips together and frowned. "Oh."

"Yeah. Oh." She returned to the sofa and sank down. "I'm totally ruined. I'll have to close the Muffin Top and declare bankruptcy."

Sam patted Lauren's shoulder. "Something will work out. It always does."

Lauren crossed her arms. "In the meantime, I'm going to give Paul a piece of my mind."

"That's my big sister."

Both their heads swiveled toward the stairs when they heard footsteps ascending to the living room.

Paul opened his mouth to speak, but Lauren beat him to it. She sprang to her feet and waved the letter in his face.

"You didn't have the decency, the courtesy, to give me a heads up that my loan with the bank was being called?"

Paul looked shell-shocked. "I—"

"And you didn't bother to mention that you're the President and CEO?" Lauren spat the words at him.

Paul gave a sheepish shrug. "I thought it sounded better than 'owner.'"

Lauren hissed out a breath. "How dare you lead me on with sweet words and kisses when all along you planned to ruin me financially."

Sam's eyebrows rose at the word 'kiss.' Lauren spared her a glance before facing Paul again. "I can't run out and apply for another loan. My identity was stolen, remember? You've ruined my life." These last words were choked out through her tear-thickened throat.

"I'm sorry." Paul seemed to be saying those words a lot lately. He'd finally gotten Marvin to come out of the room where he'd escaped to. Paul's apology seemed to mollify the man. They'd briefly talked about what they could do about the car situation. They'd decided to make the best of the situation by telling the ladies they might have to spend the night there.

He'd forgotten about the SBA announcement going out the previous week. With everything he had going on, Paul had forgotten to talk to Lauren. Now he was kicking himself for never actually telling her what he was doing in Hornell generally, and at First Upstate Bank specifically.

The result was this woman he was coming to care deeply about was mad enough to strangle him.

"Sorry won't cut it," Lauren said, turning her back on him.

He reached out to grab her arm, but she jerked away.

Marvin reached the top of the stairs and spoke from behind him. "Did you let the ladies know . . ."

His voice trailed off. The tension was thick as the sheets of rain blowing across the wood deck.

Samantha stood and faced him. "He told us all right. Your boss wrote it in a letter. How he plans to bankrupt my sister."

Paul had to fix this. "I'll give you the money to cover the SBA loan."

The only sound in the room was the pounding of the rain. No one spoke for what felt like an hour.

"You're kidding, right?" Lauren asked. Her face was an angry mask.

"Or I could loan it to you," Paul offered, holding out a placating hand.

Lauren made a sound of disgust. "Unbelievable. You think all your billions of dollars can fix anything. Well, you can't fix this."

Paul opened his mouth to say something. Before he could form the words, the room went dark.

Marin stepped around him. "Looks like the power's out."

Paul rubbed his hands over his cheeks. Could this day get any worse?

# Chapter 23

**Lauren and Samantha** huddled on one sofa, wrapped in a thick blanket. The light outside was fading into dusk. The intense rain had diminished to a slight drizzle. Paul had disappeared somewhere. Lauren didn't care. Marvin kept them updated on the power and cell phone situation each time he fed logs into the massive stone fireplace.

"My source reports the power should be restored by midnight," he said, brushing his hands off. "Can I get you ladies anything?"

"A ride out of here," Lauren said under her breath.

"I'm working on that." Marvin's smile seemed forced.

"Your boss is a horse's ass," Sam said. Lauren elbowed her under the blanket.

"He can be. But he is also incredible generous. He meant what he said about lending you the money."

Lauren snorted. "Yeah, no."

Marvin lowered himself onto the edge of the coffee table. "Did he ever tell you how we met?"

Lauren shook her head.

Marvin's gaze focused on a point over Lauren's head. "After I got out of prison, I was a hot mess. Five years is a long time to be incarcerated. Not to mention, it's pretty darn impossible to get a job when you're a felon. Long story short, I ended up homeless, as many of us do."

"I'm sorry," muttered Lauren.

"That's not the end of the story." Marvin's voice lowered. "I was panhandling in Manhattan, and Mr. Montrose hit me with his car. He could have driven away. I mean, hitting a homeless man in New York is almost a sport for some folks. But he pulled over and stayed with me until an ambulance came. Rather than brush his hands off and consider the deed done, he followed the ambulance to the hospital."

By now, Lauren and Samantha had straightened and were leaning forward to hear the rest of Marvin's story.

"When Mr. Montrose found out I had no family to speak of, he not only paid my entire hospital bill, but when I was able to be released, he offered me a job as his assistant."

Marvin pinned Lauren with his eyes. "I'm the reason he doesn't drive."

Lauren sucked in a breath. "I-I don't know what to say."

"The thing is, Miss Lauren, he could have left me in the street that day. He could have paid my bill and gone on his merry way. But he didn't. I may be the reason he refuses to drive to this day. But he's the reason I'm sitting here today."

Marvin stood and stretched. "So maybe you can cut him a little slack?"

Sam spoke up. "What about the loan stuff? Couldn't he have at least said something to my sister?"

Marvin sighed. "You have no idea what it's like

managing the many projects Mr. Montrose has. Sometimes he forgets things." He shrugged. "This is one of those times. I can assure you, it wasn't because he wanted to hurt your sister."

Marvin checked the fire, poked at it, and walked outside to grab another handful of logs.

Lauren exchanged a look with Samantha. She watched Marvin with lowered eyelashes until he disappeared into one of the other rooms upstairs.

"Wow," Lauren said.

"I can't even," Sam answered.

"Now I feel bad."

Sam leaned back against the cushions. "Maybe you should give him another chance?"

Before Lauren could answer, the lights flickered once and came on.

"Hallelujah," Lauren exclaimed.

Sam shot her a look. "We're still stuck here until we get another car."

Lauren's joy fizzled. "Oh, yeah."

Paul bounded up the stairs, anxious to share the news.

"I finally got hold of someone in my New York office. A car should be here shortly." He avoided direct eye contact with Lauren. Was she still mad? Most likely. He'd let her down in a big way.

Neither women spoke. Paul retreated to the kitchen and pulled open the subzero refrigerator. He pulled lunchmeat and cheese from the meat drawer and set it on the counter.

"Anybody want a sandwich?" he called into the living room.

No answer.

He'd regret this sandwich later, but right now Paul needed comfort food. And lots of it. Why was he such a git? In the space of a few hours, he'd angered his assistant and alienated Lauren and her sister.

No one would call him an underachiever, that was for sure.

Rain on the road outside the kitchen window reflected the dim light shining from the moon. Paul devoured his sandwich in a few bites, regretting his decision to eat. Instead of the rush of dopamine, his stomach churned. It would be cosmic retribution if he ended up with an ulcer. Would it be weird if he threw up what he'd just eaten?

A double tap on a car horn brought his attention back to the window. A vehicle pulled up to the house and the dome light came on as a man climbed out. Flooded with a sense of relief, he pulled open the door and motioned the man inside.

"Mr. Montrose?"

"I'm Montrose. Thank you for coming all this way. As you may have seen, my current vehicle is undriveable."

"Not a problem. I'm happy to help."

Marvin appeared at the top of the stairs shrugging into his suit coat. He and the driver shook hands.

Lauren and Samantha soon crowded into the kitchen, carrying their handbags.

"Is everyone ready?" Marvin asked.

Paul noted the relief in their voices as they said yes.

"I'll stay with the car, Mr. Montrose," Marvin said.

"A tow truck is on its way."

"You don't have to do that," Paul said. "We can deal with it tomorrow."

"If it's all the same to you, I'd prefer to wait here. I'll arrange for a ride back to Hornell later."

Paul glanced at his Rolex. "But it's already late."

"Still," Marvin said.

Paul shrugged and huffed in frustration. "Fine."

"Right this way, ladies," the driver said. "I'm Aaron. Let's get you back home, shall we?"

Aaron opened the back door of the sedan, and the women climbed in. Paul sighed. He'd be stuck having to make nice to the new guy in the front seat.

With a final wave to Marvin standing on the front porch, Aaron pointed the car toward home.

"Quite the storm," Aaron said.

"Indeed." The storm outside was nothing compared to the storm back in the house they'd left. Between his tussle with Marvin and Lauren's rage, Paul was ready to crawl into a hole, lick his wounds, and whatever other cliches he could pull out.

"You ladies warm enough back there?" Aaron asked, glancing over his shoulder.

"Fine."

This was not going to be a fun ride home. How had the situation come to this?

*Because you're a stupid twit. You should have told Lauren you'd bought the bank. You should have considered what it would do for her to lose the bank's funding. You should have . . .*

Paul remembered Da's words of wisdom. 'Instead of dwelling on what's done, think about how you can fix it.'

Was his relationship with Lauren fixable? A plan began to form as the car ate up the miles toward Hornell.

# Chapter 24

Lauren gripped the door handle like a lifeline. The minute the vehicle stopped, she jumped out. "Thanks for the ride," she said and slammed the door closed. Thank goodness Paul didn't try to stop her.

She led Sam up the stairs to the apartment and unlocked the door. "I'm exhausted," she said, dropping her purse on the kitchen table.

Sam stretched and yawned. "Yeah. It's exhausting having someone feed you and drive you places."

"Sarcasm does not become you," Lauren said. "I need to call Kennedy. Maybe she'll keep Molly overnight."

Sam grabbed pajamas from her open suitcase and headed toward the bathroom. "I don't know why you took on that responsibility. Don't you have enough on your plate as it is?"

"It seemed like a good idea at the time. You know, fostering a service puppy to help some disabled person. Or maybe a veteran suffering from PTSD? I watched a documentary, and it looked good." Her voice trailed off. Sam was right. Molly was a responsibility she'd have to deal with if she had to close the Muffin Top.

She sank onto the sofa with a sigh and stretched her

legs out on the coffee table. "What am I going to do?" Guilt, embarrassment, and self-doubt flooded in like an old friend. Her brain refused to shut off the chatter. Was Molly an attempt to feel valuable? After her ex dumped her for being 'too fat,' she'd pulled the remains of her shredded self-esteem around her and tried to power through the hurt.

Faced with another man's betrayal was the last straw.

"I'm going to remain single forever," she said aloud.

Sam returned to the living room in her cotton pajamas. "You're going to what?"

Devoid of makeup, her sister was still beautiful. Natural ash blonde hair and cheekbones to die for. Even if Lauren lost sixty pounds, she'd never have that bone structure. Sam was a carbon copy of their mother while Lauren resembled their dad. She was curves, and Samantha was angles.

"Be single forever. I'll be the crazy cat lady."

"You'll have to get a cat first."

"You're a buzz kill, you know that?"

Sam grinned. "That's my middle name."

Sam was studying her phone screen when Lauren's lit up with an incoming call. She moaned and held the phone up to Sam. "It's Mom."

"Better answer it. Otherwise, she'll hang up and call me."

Lauren pressed her lips together and punched the green button. "Hi, Mom."

"Is Sam with you?" Mom asked.

"I'm here," Sam answered.

"Oh, good. I get to talk to both of my girls. Are you

two having fun together?"

Lauren exchanged a look with her sister. "Yeah, fun." If you could call getting bad news from the bank 'fun.' And finding out your almost boyfriend stabbed you in the back.

"What did you do today?" Mom asked.

Lauren leaned toward Sam and whispered, "Your turn."

"We had a nice time. Lauren's friend took us to Keuka Lake to see the house he's remodeling."

"A man? Lauren has a friend who's a man?"

Lauren rolled her eyes, causing Sam to smother a giggle.

"Yes, Mom. Lauren has a male friend."

"Is he handsome? Rich? How good of a friend is he, Lauren?"

Now Sam rolled her eyes. "He's handsome."

Lauren leaned over to speak into the phone. "He's a customer, Mom. Not even a good friend."

"Well, maybe he would be interested in Samantha?"

"Mom—" Lauren said.

"I'm not getting any younger, you know. And neither are you two. I want to see you settled down like your brother."

Lauren shook her head and exchanged a glance with Sam.

"Sure, Mom. We'll get on that right away."

"Lauren," Mom warned. "Don't get sassy. You know men aren't attracted to sarcastic women. Nor fat ones."

"And here we go," Lauren said, shoving the phone toward her sister.

Sam took the phone from Lauren. "Mom, stop. Quit

with the body shaming."

"You of all people should know that you have to make yourself attractive."

Sam sighed. "Sure, Mom. Whatever you say."

Lauren made a slashing motion across her neck. Sam nodded. "Mom, we have to go. Lauren's oven timer is going off." Sam hit the disconnect button and tossed the phone onto the sofa cushion.

"I'm gonna go shower," Lauren said.

Before she could get to her feet, Sam grabbed her arm. "Don't let her get to you."

"Too late." Lauren escaped to the bathroom and leaned her arms on the counter. Raising her head, she peered at herself in the mirror. A round face stared back at her. Mom was right. She was fat.

Paul hadn't seemed to mind her size. He'd barely spared her willowy sister a glance.

"Yeah, but thanks to him, I'm going to be broke and homeless," she said to her reflection.

The nerve of him saying he'd give or lend her the money to pay off the bank loan. She was proud of making it thus far without asking for help from Mom and Dad. She didn't need a white knight to swoop in and save the day. What she needed was a solution out of this current situation.

Paul's New York City attorney had taken on her identity theft case. She assured Lauren with time it would all be straightened out. Time wasn't on Lauren's side. The letter from Mr. Paul Montrose, President and CEO gave her sixty days to find an alternative source of funding. Or lose everything.

After showering, Lauren returned to the living room to find Samantha pacing from the kitchen to the end of the living room and back, phone pressed to her ear.

"What's going on?" she mouthed. Sam's face was white when she disconnected.

"I've gotta leave tomorrow."

"Why? Why happened?"

Sam sank onto the sofa and buried her face in her hands. Her eyes were frantic when she looked up. "That was my agent. She's been monitoring my mail. I got another letter from the stalker. He's escalating and she wants me to go to the police first thing Monday morning."

Lauren sat next to her and gathered Sam into a hug. "Oh, honey, I'm so sorry. Are you all right?"

"Yes. No. I don't know." Sam's voice was muffled against Lauren's shoulder.

"I wanted to have a nice, relaxing weekend with you and now it's ruined."

Lauren rubbed circles on Sam's back. "This isn't your fault. If anything, it was mine for making you go with me to Paul's house. Look how that turned out."

When Sam pulled away, her face was streaked with tears. "We're a couple of hot messes, aren't we?"

Lauren nodded with a wry smile. Her smile faded when she thought about her sister being stalked by a crazy person. "Be careful, okay?"

"I will. My agent thinks I should cancel some of my upcoming contracts. Maybe take some time off."

"That sounds like a good idea."

"You don't understand the modeling business. It's out of sight, out of mind. If I go into hiding, it'll be difficult to get back on everyone's radar."

"Isn't that why you pay your agent?"

"She isn't a miracle worker."

"Yeah, but if your stalker finds you ..." Lauren let her voice trail off.

Sam scrubbed the tears from her cheeks with the edge of her pajama top. "I know." She sighed. "Better an uphill climb getting back than dead."

"Dead?"

Sam nodded slowly. "Yeah, his latest letter was threatening."

"Oh, my gosh, Sam. Be careful."

"I will, Sis. I will."

Paul woke early after a night of tossing and turning on his memory foam bed. He was alone in the house. Marvin's bedroom door stood open, and his bed was untouched.

"Bugger," Paul muttered.

Another of Paul's employees had met Aaron at the rental, leaving the unassuming sedan in the driveway. Where was Marvin? Paul's stomach tumbled with fear that Marvin had quit.

Paul chewed two antacids and brewed himself a cup of tea while he waited for the medicine to settle his stomach. He'd come up with a plan to make things right with Lauren during the night. But in the bright light of morning, it seemed weak and pathetic.

He missed his Da. He'd have some words of wisdom in this situation. What would his dad do? Turn to his Bible, that's what.

Paul searched his bedroom for the Bible his parents had given him years ago. He found it in the back of a bureau drawer under some tee shirts. He carried it to the kitchen and sat at the table.

Where to begin to read? Da had loved the book of Proverbs. Paul thumbed through the pages until he found the book.

He scanned chapters one and two until his attention was caught by Proverbs 3:27. "Do not withhold good from those to whom it is due, when it is in the power of your hand to do so."

Paul took a sip of his lukewarm tea, letting the words sink into his heart. Perhaps the plan he'd devised in the middle of the night wasn't weak and pathetic at all. It could work. But not until Monday when financial institutions were open.

He could, however, make some phone calls.

Paul's phone chirped with a text from Marvin.

**Marvin**: The car situation is taking longer than expected. Won't be back until tomorrow. Movers arriving Tuesday to the rental. Let me know if you need anything.

That explained Marvin's absence. Until Marvin returned, he was stuck in the house.

"Blast," Paul said aloud. He tapped a response.

**Paul**: What time tomorrow?

**Marvin**: Not sure. I will let you know.

"Bugger." If Marvin didn't arrive in the morning, Paul would be stuck. No way would he get behind the wheel of the sedan. His stomach again kicked up acid, spreading the burning up his esophagus.

He had to make things right with Lauren. And Marvin.

After yesterday's squall, the sky seemed to be relieved to be clear again. Hot mist hovered over the grass, clogging Paul's lungs. He grabbed a breath and was transported back to his homeland. Upstate New York summers could hold their own in a competition for humidity. Especially today, when moisture from the rain pushed its way into the morning air.

"Eish, it's going to be a hot one today."

Pushing back his chair, he stepped to the sliding glass door. The rented Air B&B was a small island of comfort. Except for the presence of another human, the place was perfect. He hadn't had the opportunity to talk with Marvin about having him stay here. The accident with the fallen tree eliminated the chance to offer the rental to him once the sale was finalized.

Would Marvin see his offer as a bribe, something to make amends for being such a git? Lauren had spurned his offer of financial help for her current situation. What was the use of having all this money if he wasn't able to help others?

The sermon from Lauren's church last week echoed in his brain. "And again I say to you, it is easier for a camel to go through the eye of a needle than for a rich man to enter the kingdom of God."

If that was the case, what chance did he have?

# Chapter 25

**Samantha clambered down** Lauren's apartment stairs leaving behind a cloud of fragrance. Lauren waved goodbye as her sister got into her car and drove away. Instead of church, Lauren went back to bed. Her sleep had been filled with anxious dreams about Sam's stalker and her own uncertain future.

Worst case scenario, she could move back in with her parents until she figured out what to do.

"Ugh." Living under the same roof with her mom would be a train wreck. "There has to be a solution," Lauren said to the ceiling. "God? Are you listening?"

She fell into a deep sleep and woke feeling only slightly refreshed. Kennedy would be there soon to deliver Molly.

A text came from Sam.

**Sam**: Home safe. Talk later. This was followed by a heart emoji.

Lauren sent a thumbs up.

She busied herself straightening up after her sister's visit, tossing sheets and towels into the washer. Kennedy tapped on the door when Lauren gave a last swipe of a rag on the bathroom counter.

"Hey, there you are," Lauren said, opening the door. Molly rushed in and planted her paws on Lauren's chest. "No, you don't, young lady. Down."

"She was a perfect angel with us," Kennedy said. "William adores her. I may have to break down and get him a dog."

Lauren sent her a rueful smile. "If things don't work out with the service dog agency, maybe they'll let you take her."

Kennedy leaned down to scratch between Molly's ears. "That would be great. William is finally coming out of his shell."

"Less snarly?"

"Oh, yeah. But enough about me. How was your time with Mr. Hot South Africa?"

Lauren's mouth turned down. "Ugh. First, the storm was intense, and a huge tree came down on the car. we had to wait for someone to show up with another car. Then the power went out."

"Sounds cozy."

"Anything but. You will never believe the letter I got from the bank."

"Wait, you got a letter while you were headed to Keuka Lake?"

"You better sit down," Lauren said, pointing to the sofa.

"Remember how you handed me the mail when we were leaving? I didn't look at anything until we were sitting in the semi-darkness waiting for either the power to come on or a car to arrive."

Lauren unfolded the letter sitting on the coffee table and handed it to Kennedy. She waited while her employee scanned the letter before setting it on the sofa between them.

"What does this mean for the Muffin Top?"

"I don't know yet. I doubt I can get another loan. Whoever stole my identity ruined my credit. My score is in the high five hundreds now." Lauren snatched up the letter and thrust it in Kennedy's direction.

"The bigger issue is this." She pointed to the signature line.

Kennedy's brow crinkled. "I don't understand."

Lauren huffed in frustration. "See the signature? Mr. Paul Montrose, President and CEO," her voice dripped sarcasm. "He is your Mr. Hot South Africa."

Kennedy gasped and put a hand to her face. "No way. Why would he do that to you?"

Lauren hung her head. "I don't know, Ken. That is a great question."

"I thought he liked you."

"Ha. I thought so too. Guess not."

Kennedy made a sound of disgust.

"Why do guys from South African all turn out to be jerks?" Lauren said.

"Wait, what? You better give me some deets, Boss."

Lauren sighed. "Before you started working here, I was going out with this guy. He broke up with me because I wouldn't sleep with him."

"Total dirt bag," Kennedy said.

"He was also from South Africa."

"Ah. I see how you recognized that accent."

Lauren and Kennedy leaned back against the cushions and stretched their legs out onto the coffee table, lost in their own thoughts. After a few minutes, Kennedy got to her feet.

"I better get home and make sure William hasn't been doing something he shouldn't. Did I tell you I caught him smoking the other day?"

Lauren stood and pulled Kennedy in for a hug. "Bless you for taking on that responsibility. In case anyone hasn't told you lately, you're doing a great job with William."

"Thanks. I needed that." Kennedy gave Molly one last pat and headed out the door.

After Kennedy left, Lauren sat at her table and pulled her laptop close. "Time to do some searching," she said to Molly.

She typed 'alternative business financing' into the search bar and was soon lost in research.

Two hours later, Lauren stood, stretched, and reached for Molly's sleeping form.

"C'mon, girl, let's get some fresh air."

They headed down the stairs and outside to the yard. Thick air assaulted her.

"Holy smokes, it's humid today."

Molly didn't seem to be affected. Lauren put a hand on her chest and sucked in the humid air. Yesterday's squall left enough moisture in the air to create a sauna.

Her phone buzzed, and her brother's face filled the screen.

"Hi, David. You never call me. Is everything okay?"

Her brother's laugh sounded loud in the speaker. "Everything's fine. I wanted to let you know Jeanie is pregnant again."

"Mom told me. Congratulations." Did her enthusiasm sound forced? Probably. "That's great.

When is she due?"

"Around Christmas."

"Cool." What was David's motive for calling? Their relationship wasn't like hers and Sam's. He must have an ulterior motive. She held her breath, waiting.

"The thing is, Lauren, I wanted to talk to you about moving down here to Florida."

"What? Why?"

"Well, Mom and Dad are here. And Jeanie and I are, too. I feel bad you're up there in New York by yourself."

"Sam's here."

"Yeah, but she travels all the time. Besides, she's in The City and you're there in Hornell."

"David, I have a business here. I'm established." But was she? If she couldn't get financing, she'd have to let the business go. Was this God's way of throwing her a lifeline?

"You could sell the business and start a new one down here." David's tone changed. "Besides, we could use your help."

And there it was. Just like Mom, David had a reason for calling that had nothing to do with brotherly love.

"What kind of help, David?"

"Jeanie is having a difficult pregnancy. She's supposed to take it easy for the next five months. We need help with Ryan and Kelsey."

"So, you expect me to close my business, move to Florida, and become a nanny to your kids? You can't be serious."

How was it possible Mom and Dad had spawned such an insufferable jerk?

"Could you get someone to run the bakery for you?

It's only a few months, Lauren. Think about how fun it would be to get to know your niece and nephew better."

Before Lauren could form a response, David hit her with a final blow. "Mom and Dad aren't getting any younger, you know. They could use some help, too."

Lauren swallowed a laugh. The last time she'd talked to their dad, he'd sounded fine, bragging about how he'd lowered his golf handicap. And Mom spent her days playing pickle ball. They were nowhere near their deathbeds.

"David, while your offer sounds great," Lauren choked on the lie, "I can't see myself uprooting here and moving to Florida. You and Jeanie will have to work this out yourselves. Without me."

Lauren disconnected, proud she'd held her ground. "Come on, Molly, let's go back inside where it's cool."

Upstairs in her apartment, Lauren opened her freezer and pulled out the chocolate chip cookie dough she'd frozen several weeks ago.

"Time for some rage baking." And eating.

Monday morning dawned with another cloudless day. Paul peered out the window to the sedan sitting like a hulking predator on the driveway. Sweat prickled his palms. Could his need to get to the bank override his terror over climbing behind the wheel of the car?

He remembered the sound of his vehicle striking Marvin. The sickening thud of metal colliding with flesh and bone. The incident still haunted his dreams. A therapist told him to 'get back out there and try again.' Like riding a bicycle. Or mounting a horse after getting thrown.

If only it were that simple. Letting go of the past was easier said than done.

Maybe he should walk to the bank. But one step outside squashed that thought. The humidity was enough to push him back into the cool interior. Walking would mean he'd arrive at work sweating like a pig.

The car keys hung on a hook by the door like a viper waiting to strike. He smoothed sweaty hands down his thighs, softening the knife-edge pleats.

An inhale, then, "You can do this."

His phone chirped and he jumped.

**Marvin**: Got held up in The City. Back after three.

"Buggers." Paul reached for the keys, snatching them free from the hook. "Don't be a twit."

His hand shook as he locked the door to the Air B&B. Turning, he faced the sedan, sweat already trickling down his spine.

Another inhale, then he stumbled down the steps with legs like cooked pasta.

The door opened easily.

"You can do this. You will do this." Overhead, birds circled and danced with carefree abandon. How he envied them at that moment.

*Get in the car.*

He swung the door closed and snapped the seatbelt. Resting both hands on the steering wheel, Paul tried to keep the churning nausea at bay.

He exhaled and pressed the Start button. The car purred to life. Paul swallowed against the bile rising in his throat and put the car in reverse.

He let momentum carry the sedan out of the driveway. Jamming on the brake, he jerked the car to a rocking stop. Resting his forehead on the steering wheel, Paul waited for his pulse to return to a semblance of normal.

When that didn't happen, he shifted into drive and returned the car to its previous position. Opening the door, he leaned out and threw up on the gravel driveway.

Time to try again.

Keeping the sedan at a crawl, he drove the few miles to downtown Hornell. The streets were deserted this early, and for that Paul was grateful. He arrived at the bank and pulled to a stop, congratulating himself for the small victory. Wiping sweaty hands on his slacks, he opened the door and stepped out of the car. His legs felt like he'd run a half marathon. He wobbled into the bank and set to work.

"Carol, I have my phone on do not disturb. Unless the building is on fire or there's a robbery, I'm going to be unavailable for a couple of hours."

Carol nodded and returned to her computer.

After numerous phone calls and emails, Paul armed himself with a sheaf of papers.

"Carol, I'm going out for a bit. If you need me, I'll be available via text."

"Sure thing, Paul," Carol said, glancing up from her computer.

He loosened his tie as he exited the bank. The sun warmed the sidewalk and heated Paul's shoulders. By the time he arrived at Lauren's place, sweat moistened his back. He paused at the gate leading into her yard. He remembered the door to her apartment was around the side of the building and up a set of stairs.

He pushed open the gate and stopped in his tracks.

Who was that man casually sitting next to Lauren on a lounge chair with his hand on her arm?

# Chapter 26

"**Let's go outside** and enjoy some of this sunshine," Lauren said, leading Molly down the stairs. After throwing the ball for a rousing game of fetch, Lauren sank onto a lounge chair and stretched out her legs.

The sun warmed her skin and helped calm her brain. After hours of searching, Lauren felt confident she could find a loan to replace the SBA loan on the business. It would be expensive, but with a little luck and God's grace, she could make it. Well, that and take on more catering clients.

"This might be the last Monday off," she said to Molly. The pup panted her agreement. "Yeah, I know it's hot, but the sun will do us both some good."

Lauren turned as the sound of approaching footsteps caught her attention. Shading her eyes against the glare, she watched as a familiar figure ambled toward her.

"Hello, love."

A jolt of adrenaline shot from head to toe. "Nigel, what are you doing here?" How dare her ex show up unannounced.

"Long time no see, Lauren," he said, perching on the edge of the lounger.

Lauren clenched her fists, fighting the urge to punch his smug face. How had she ever thought 'him whose name won't be uttered' was handsome?

"I was in the area and thought I'd check on my favorite girl."

Lauren inhaled through clenched teeth. "I am not your favorite girl. And I don't think I ever was, Nigel."

His laugh grated on Lauren's last nerve. "Oh, come on, love. Don't be like that. We had some good times."

Yeah, until you said I was fat.

"What is it you want, Nigel?"

Molly raised her head and growled.

"What a scary guard dog you have. What's its name?"

Before Lauren could answer, an angry voice split the air. "What the bloody hell are you doing here?"

Lauren straightened to see Paul charging toward them, his face dark with fury.

"Hello, Paul. Fancy meeting you here."

Lauren's head swung from her ex to Paul and back. "You two know each other?"

Paul stopped in front of Nigel and spit the words at Nigel's smirking face.

"He's my brother."

Lauren sprang to her feet. "Brother?" She laid a hand on her heart beating painfully against her ribs. "But your last name isn't Montrose."

"Half-brother," corrected Nigel.

Lauren leaned over to counter the sudden wave of vertigo. "I think I'm going to be sick."

Paul grabbed Lauren's arm to steady her and gently lowered her to the lounger.

"Breathe," he commanded.

Nigel stood with his hands jammed in his designer jeans pockets. Paul looked him up and down, noting the superb fit of his silk shirt and the Italian leather shoes. Clothes that Paul had probably bought with the money he'd sent.

His mouth turned down in disgust. His half-brother was the git who'd hurt Lauren? As soon as he got her settled, he would punch Nigel in the nose.

"I see you've met my girlfriend," Nigel said, rising on his toes and back down.

Rage pushed its way from Paul's chest and clouded his vision. He clenched his fists at his sides to keep from taking a swing.

Nigel seemed unaware of the possibility of a broken nose. "I heard you were in this little village, and I thought," he snapped his fingers, "I know someone in Hornell. I should go and see what's what."

Paul glanced down at Lauren, who held her head with both hands.

"What's what," Paul repeated.

Nigel smiled. "Exactly."

"What's what is you can get yourself out of here before I throttle you."

Nigel threw back his head and laughed. "I don't think Lauren would appreciate you slugging her boyfriend. After all—"

"You're not my boyfriend," Lauren protested.

"Don't be like that, love," Nigel said. He rested a hand on her shoulder. "I know, I should never have left you the way I did. I'll make it up to you. I promise."

"Get your hand off her," Paul warned.

"Or what, little brother?" Nigel challenged him with a look. "It's more than my hand that's been on her. Did she tell you we were very close—"

Before Nigel finished his sentence, Paul's fist rose of its own volition and connected with Nigel's face with a satisfying crunch.

'Ow!" Nigel clapped a hand to his reddening cheek.

"Stop it you two," Lauren said. She struggled to her feet and faced them.

Paul reached a hand to her, letting it drop when she cringed.

"Nigel, you are not welcome here. Not ever." She turned to Paul. "Why are you here?"

Paul leaned over to pick up the sheaf of papers he'd dropped. "Never mind."

Nigel opened his mouth to speak but Lauren cut him off. "Just go. Both of you."

Paul waited for Nigel to move toward the gate. One glance back at Lauren's angry face before he followed his brother out of Lauren's yard.

When they reached the sidewalk, Nigel stopped and turned.

"You should ask him how he became so rich," Nigel said, hooking a thumb at Paul. "Ask him about our dad's death."

Paul briefly closed his eyes. It was just like Nigel to bring up the tragic accident that had taken his parents.

Nigel fell into step with Paul as they walked down the sidewalk in the direction of the bank.

"You pack a hefty punch, mate," Nigel said, fingering his jaw.

"Apparently not hefty enough to shut your mouth."

Nigel laugh was followed by ouch.

Paul halted and turned toward his brother. "What was that business back there?"

"Just having a little fun."

Paul was going to punch him again. "Fun? At Lauren's expense?"

Nigel shrugged. "If I'd known you were that into her … "

"You'd what? Let her be? Or cause even more trouble?"

Nigel's shrug said it all.

"Look, mate, bugger off. Go back to whatever hole you crawled out of and don't come back."

"I didn't know you were into fat girls."

Paul wanted to smack the smug look from his half-brother's face. "She isn't fat." Pleasantly round. Full-figured. Womanly. Paul resumed his walk with Nigel a step behind.

"Have you shagged her yet?"

His steps ground to a halt. Paul whirled to face him. "You disgust me."

Nigel raised his hands in surrender. "It's a fair question."

"How our dad managed to spawn such a git is a mystery."

Nigel's face twisted. "If 'our dad' hadn't given me away, maybe I'd have turned out differently. You're the one who got all the breaks. You're the golden boy who could do no wrong. Dad couldn't be bothered to acknowledge me."

"Until he did." Paul studied Nigel's face for a scrap of decency.

"Fat lot of good it did me. By then you were firmly

ensconced as the heir. Did you cause the accident that killed them so you could have it all?"

Paul let his fist fly, catching Nigel under his jaw. Nigel went down, arms flailing as the sidewalk rose to meet him. Nigel groaned and struggled to sit. Paul kicked him in the ribs.

"Do not. Ever. Talk to me again."

A small crowd had gathered on the sidewalk, some with cell phones held aloft filming the altercation.

Paul pulled at his cufflinks and straightened his suit jacket. "It's over, folks." He left Nigel writhing on the sidewalk as he strode toward the bank.

An hour later, two uniformed policemen entered the lobby. Paul rose from his desk to greet them, cradling his sore hand.

"Come into my office, gentlemen," Paul said, leaving Carol gawking from her desk.

"Mr. Montrose, I'm Officer Morris and this is Officer Spykerman."

Paul smiled, hoping to diffuse the sudden tension. "Spykerman sounds like a South African name."

Officer Spykerman smiled. "My grandparents emigrated to the US before I was born."

"Ah. My parents left for England when I was younger. I've been in the States about two years."

"Do you know why we're here?" Morris asked.

"To open a checking account?" Paul's attempt at humor fell flat.

"Your brother—"

"Half-brother."

Morris cleared his throat. "Your half-brother is Nigel Kimani, correct?"

"That is correct."

"Mr. Kimani states you physically assaulted him."

"That is also correct."

"He is pressing charges," Spykerman said.

"That's preposterous." Paul crossed his arms and pushed his shoulders back.

"That may be so, but would you mind coming down to the police station with us so we can sort this out?"

Paul barked out a laugh. "Yes, I mind."

Morris reached behind his back and pulled out a set of handcuffs. Dangling them, he said, "Would you rather willingly come with us or …"

Paul closed his eyes and exhaled. "Fine."

He paused by Carol's desk. "Carol, I'm going out for a bit. I'm not sure when I'll be back." A glance around the lobby showed his employees staring wide-eyed at the drama unfolding.

"Of course," Carol replied without making eye contact.

Spykerman opened the back door of the patrol car, and Paul climbed in.

At least he didn't have to drive. He was still a bit shaken over his morning commute to the bank.

The drive to the Hornell Police Department was mercifully short. Paul breathed through his mouth to avoid the rank smell of old vomit and sweat. His suit would likely reek as well.

"May I text my assistant?" Paul asked, leaning forward to speak through the wire grill separating the front from the back.

"That's fine."

Paul pulled out his phone and sent a quick text to Marvin.

**Paul**: If you're back in town, please meet me at the

police station.

Before he could add any more, the car jerked to a halt in the parking area behind the police department. Paul was ushered into the building and led to a holding room.

"Please wait here," Morris instructed.

"I'd like an attorney, please," Paul said.

Morris rolled his eyes and glanced at his partner. "You aren't under arrest, Mr. Montrose."

Not yet, came the implied intent.

# Chapter 27

**Paul drummed his** aching fingers on the metal table. His quick temper had gotten the better of him yet again. Part of him wished he'd murdered his half-brother. Nigel had been a pain in his backside since he'd appeared at Da's funeral with his hand out.

"I want what's mine," Nigel had demanded.

Nigel felt he was entitled to half of his parents' estate and planned to go to court to contest the will. At the time, Paul thought it best to offer Nigel enough money to get him out of his hair.

Like a stray cat you feed once, he kept coming back for more. Every time one of his shady business deals fell flat, Nigel magically appeared, expecting Paul to 'do the right thing.'

If only Da had told Paul he had a half-brother. Finding out at the funeral was a double shock. Da had a fling prior to meeting Mom, resulting in the woman's pregnancy. She'd gotten married and her husband wanted to raise Nigel as his own. It wasn't until Nigel needed a passport to leave South Africa that he discovered the man he'd called father wasn't his biological dad.

Like a wolf smelling his prey, Nigel followed the

money trail leading up to Paul's inheritance. As Paul's wealth grew, Nigel's avarice grew along with it. Paul continued to give Nigel money out of guilt.

Paul swallowed against the acid churning in his stomach. What he wouldn't give for a drink of water. If he wasn't under arrest, why was he still sitting in this hot room?

Paul scooted the metal chair back and stood. He rattled the doorknob. Locked. He pounded on the door, regretting the decision when his bruised fist reminded him of the blow to Nigel's jaw.

Pacing the small room, his thoughts returned to Nigel's disgusting comments about Lauren. Had they been as intimate as Nigel hinted? Had he been wrong about her?

He patted his jacket pocket searching for the antacids he kept there. He chewed two and prayed they'd work quickly.

The door swung open, and Morris stepped into the room. "Mr. Montrose, will you come with me please?"

"Where are we going?" Hopefully not to a jail cell. He wasn't familiar with how the laws in America worked. Wasn't he supposed to have his rights read? And have a lawyer present?

"Your brother has agreed to drop the charges, but he wants to speak with you first."

Paul's spirits rose and fell. How much would this cost him?

Officer Morris led Paul to a small office. Nigel rose from his seat when Paul entered. Paul noted with satisfaction the darkening skin around Nigel's eye and the lump on his jaw.

"I'll leave you two alone," Morris said.

Nigel eyed him warily before returning to his seat.

"What do you want, Nigel?" Paul sat and crossed his arms.

No hesitation in his quick response. "A hundred thousand."

Paul inhaled through his nose and exhaled. "No."

"Oh, come on, mate. It's a drop in the bucket for you."

"A hundred thousand this time. What about the next time?"

Nigel shrugged. "Who knows?" He leaned forward and rested his hands on his thighs. "You owe me."

"Haven't I paid you enough already?" A vein throbbed in his head reminding him of his blood pressure issues.

Nigel leaned back. "From what I see, it will never be enough. You caused our dad's accident and robbed me of the chance to get to know him. You can't put a price on that."

"The accident wasn't my fault." Paul's protest sounded weak, even to him.

"I read the report. Dad was on his cell talking to you when he went off the road."

Paul's fists clenched. He'd beaten himself up enough that he didn't need Nigel reminding him.

"Fine. A hundred thousand. But I'll have my attorney draw up an agreement that we're done."

Nigel regarded him with narrowed eyes before thrusting out his hand to shake Paul's. Paul ignored it and stood. Straightening his jacket, he turned to leave.

Morris hovered outside the door. "Let's go up front and finish the paperwork."

Paul followed Morris down the hall, Nigel on his

heels. Once they were outside, Nigel said, "I guess I'll wait to hear from your attorney."

"I'll have my assistant reach out to you when the funds are available."

"A million thanks, brother." With a smirk, he added, "Or should I say a hundred thousand."

Marvin pulled to a stop in front of the building. Sweet relief. He could finally get away from the person he most detested.

The SUV idled at the curb when Nigel turned to go.

"What will you do?" Paul asked. Not that he cared.

Nigel appeared to consider his words. "Thought I'd go back to Lauren's. See if she'd like to pick up where we left off." Nigel made a rude gesture.

Fury rose and choked Paul's ability to speak.

"I mean, unless you want to have a go at her?" Nigel said.

The edges of Paul's vision turned red. "You disgusting—"

Before he could finish, Marvin was grabbing Paul's arm. "Get in the car, Mr. Montrose."

Nigel must have sensed and impending beat down as he twirled away and sprinted down the sidewalk.

"Good thing I showed up when I did," Marvin said. "What happened back there?" He hooked a thumb toward the door to the police department.

Paul rubbed a hand across his face. "Long story. Let's go back to the rental and I'll explain."

Marvin climbed behind the wheel. "I'm just grateful I didn't have to bail you out." He shuddered. "The po-po scares me."

"I'm glad you showed up when you did. Otherwise, I'd be back inside." Paul stretched out his bruised hand.

Marvin caught his eye in the rearview mirror. "Does that bruise on your hand have any connection to Nigel's face?"

Paul sent him a wry grin. "Yes. I hope it hurts as much as my hand does."

"What'd he want this time? And why is the sedan parked at the bank?"

Paul groaned. "It's been a long day. Let's go back to the rental and I'll tell you everything. Over a glass of wine."

"Sure thing, Mr. Montrose."

"Oh, Marvin? Call me Paul."

When the two men had gone, Lauren let her hand rest on Molly's soft head. Tall cypress trees swayed in the gentle breeze. Birds sang as they flitted from branch to branch, oblivious of the storm raging inside her.

Her head ached from trying to wrap her brain around Paul and Nigel being brothers. The thought brought another swoop of vertigo.

How dare Nigel hint their relationship had been anything but platonic? What a—the word that came to mind wasn't one found in the Bible.

"Ugh. They're two of a kind, those two," she said to her pup. Molly thumped her tail in agreement.

Nigel the jerk and Paul the destroyer of business. She shuddered, remembering the feel of Nigel's hand on her shoulder. She'd been relieved when Nigel broke up with her. But also angry and hurt. Why would he think it was okay to come back and pretend they were still together.

Obviously, there was bad blood between him and Paul. What had he hinted at about Paul's parents' deaths? Was Paul responsible?

Did she care one way or another?

Why had Paul shown up with papers in his hand?

Too many questions.

"Molly, let's go inside. I've had enough sun for today." And enough drama.

Lauren's phone rang as she stepped through the door to her apartment.

"Ms. Jensen," began Susan Kennolyn, the attorney who'd been working her identity theft case. "I need you to go to your local police department and file a report. Once you've done that, please send me the case number."

Lauren blew out an exhausted breath. "Does it have to be done today?"

Susan paused. "No. But the sooner you do, the sooner we can wrap this up."

"Fine."

Lauren disconnected and went in search of her sandals. "Sorry, girl," she said to Molly as she led the pup into her kennel. "It's only for a bit. I hope."

She grabbed her purse and keys and headed down to her car.

Lauren braked to an abrupt halt when she spied Paul and Nigel exiting the police department building. They appeared to be arguing on the sidewalk outside. She gasped when Marvin grabbed Paul's arm and shoved him into their SUV.

What in the world? She scooted down in the seat when Nigel turned. She lowered her head and pretended to search for her purse on the passenger floor.

A horn's beep snapped her upright. Nigel was nowhere in sight. Breathing a sigh of relief, she parked down the street.

"Hi, Lauren. What are you doing here?"

Lauren recognized the deputy on duty as one of her former classmates.

"Hey, Vivian. I'm here to file a police report for identity theft. My attorney emailed me the instructions."

"Let me get someone to help you." Vivian placed a call. "One of our volunteers will be here to take your report. I'm sorry you're going through that."

"Yeah." Lauren leaned into the counter. "Say, what's the deal with those two guys who just left?"

Vivian leveled a gaze at her. "I'm not supposed to say anything about what goes on here."

"Not even a hint? I know those guys. Paul Montrose and Nigel Kimani." Lauren sent her what she hoped were puppy-dog eyes.

Vivian rubbed a hand across her face and leaned forward. "All I know is one guy beat up the other and then dropped the charges." She made a slashing motion across her lips.

"Thanks. My lips are sealed."

After the way Paul had slugged Nigel's face, it wouldn't surprise her if he was the perpetrator. Could it be he was defending her reputation to her ex?

# Chapter 28

**Paul hadn't been** in to the Muffin Top for three days. *Three days.* Lauren checked her phone multiple times a day to see if he'd sent a text. Did he actually believe she'd slept with his brother?

Half-brother. Paul's voice echoed in her ear. There was a story there and she wanted to hear it.

It was probably for the best she hadn't seen him. If Paul was willing to believe she'd been intimate with Nigel, well, forget him. Besides, he was out of her league. Rich, handsome, thin. Why would he want to be with her? Unless he was merely looking for a diversion while he was in Hornell.

Or if he thought she'd be an easy conquest to satisfy him while temporarily helping at the bank.

Kennedy's voice interrupted the downward spiral of her thoughts. "I brought in the mail. More official-looking stuff from your bank."

Rather than chastise her employee for looking through her personal mail, Lauren reached for the stack of letters.

"I'll take these upstairs and check on Molly." And see in private what the bank had to say.

"Let's go outside," Lauren said when she stepped

into the apartment. Molly's body wiggled with excitement. She understood the word 'outside.'

Lauren followed her pup down the stairs and sat on the bottom step. She turned the letter from the bank over and over. "Best get it over with. Rip off the Band-Aid."

Her phone rang and Samatha's face filled the screen.

"Hey, Lauren. I wanted to let you know the latest with my crazy stalker."

Lauren's pulse sped up. "Are you okay?"

"Yes. For now, anyway." Samantha's sigh was loud in Lauren's ear. "I filed a police report, but they said there's not a lot they can do at this point. I have a couple of local shoots here in New York, nothing that's out of the studio. No live shows or anything."

"How are you feeling about that?"

"I don't know. Some days I'd like to give it all up. Throw in the proverbial towel and go back to being a normal person. Whatever that is."

"You have been modeling a long time."

"I'm trying to remember what it's like to being a regular person. To not feel like I'm on display all the time. To not be working. And dieting."

Lauren chuckled. "Try owning your own business. I work all the time too."

"I know I shouldn't complain. I make great money, and I've been to some beautiful places." Sam paused. "But just for a little while, I'd love to just be. Maybe hang out with friends in a pair of ratty sweats."

"Do you own a pair of ratty sweats?"

"You know what I mean."

"Unfortunately, I do. I wish I could help, Sam. Is

there anything I can do? Other than loan you my ratty sweats?"

"Just talking to you makes me feel better. My agent is shuffling my schedule around until this stalker situation is resolved."

"And if it isn't?"

"I'll cross that bridge when I come to it."

"In the meantime, please stay safe. I don't know what I'd do if something happened to you."

"Oh, before you hang up, did you get a call from David?"

Lauren felt a headache begin behind her left eye. "Yeah."

"I told him it was a bad idea. Was your conversation awful?"

"I hung up on him."

"Good for you. Stand your ground. And the next time Mom calls, do the same thing. Stop being a victim of Mom's verbal abuse."

If only it were that easy. Mom had a PhD in button pushing.

"Oh, I gotta go. My agent is on the other line."

Lauren disconnected, disappointed she didn't get to bring Sam up to date on the Paul/Nigel drama.

Back to the bank letter. Using a finger, she slid open the envelope and pulled out the folded sheet.

Dear Ms. Jensen:
This letter is to inform you that your loan with First Upstate Bank and The Small Business Administration has been sold to Genesee Regional Bank. Please contact the local branch at your convenience to finalize the transaction.

We hope you will enjoy the personal service you have had with First Upstate Bank.

Sincerely,
Paul Montrose
President and CEO


Well, that was a surprise. Had Paul done this just for her, or for every SBA loan?

"Only one way to find out," she said to Molly.

After Molly was back in her crate, Lauren clomped down the stairs. She waited while Kennedy finished ringing up a customer.

"Ken, can you hold down the fort? I'm going to the bank."

Kennedy raised her eyebrows. "You gonna see Paul?"

Lauren thrust her purse strap over one shoulder. "I hope so."

# Chapter 29

"That should do it," Paul said to Marvin as they sat at the table in the Air B&B.

Marvin eyed the documents he'd just signed. "I can't believe I own a house."

Paul looked away when Marvin's eyes filled with tears. "You deserve it for putting up with me."

Marvin wiped his face with the back of one hand. "Guess I can't quit now," he said, smiling through his tears.

"Guess not," Paul agreed.

"Are you ready to go?"

Paul stood and stretched. "Ready."

"Let's roll," Marvin said, jingling the keys to the new Escalade.

Paul climbed into the back seat. He rested his arm on the window, chin in hand. The passing landscape didn't bring the feeling of peace he normally experienced. Now the green pastures and tree-topped hills mocked him. Perhaps the sounds of gentle waves lapping the shore of Keuka Lake would calm the torment in his heart.

The new bank manager had been hand-picked by Chandler Daniels. His first day would be tomorrow.

Paul's work at First Upstate Bank was done. With the sale of the SBA portfolio, the bank was on its way to solvency. Any further work could be done remotely, either from his penthouse in The City, or from the new place on the lake.

Nigel's parting words had hit him harder than he expected. Nigel had always been a git, but to think he'd been with Lauren . . .

The thought made him sick. And furious. Both emotions woke him in the middle of the night and carried him into the kitchen to find comfort in unhealthy food.

Note to self—make sure Marvin doesn't leave any temptation in the lake house.

Thinking of the lake house brought back the day Lauren and her sister had come for lunch. And their kiss. Lauren's lips were soft and yielding to his. But had her lips also been on Nigel's? The thought made him nauseous.

Forget her, his mind said. Right-o, mate, his heart answered.

Marvin caught his eye in the rearview mirror. "You okay, Boss?"

"Yeah. Fine."

Marvin held his gaze before turning his attention back to the road. "Why don't I believe you?"

"Just drive."

A few minutes later, Marvin interrupted Paul's dark thoughts again. "Why not ask her? Hear it from her own words."

"It isn't that simple," Paul said with a frown.

"Sure, it is."

Paul flipped a hand. "Just drive." He wasn't about

to take advice from Marvin. What would a single man who'd been incarcerated for five years know about relationships?

Lauren thrust open the door to the bank and grabbed a breath of cold air.

"It's a hot one today," she said to Carol.

"It certainly is," Carol agreed.

Lauren pointed toward Paul's office. "Is he in?"

Carol's face clouded. "Mr. Montrose? No."

"Oh. Any idea when he'll be back?"

"I thought you knew."

Lauren shook her head. "Knew what?"

"Mr. Montrose is gone. Mr. Daniels hired a manager. He starts tomorrow."

Lauren's heart fell to her open-toed sandals. "Gone? Where?"

Carol's shrug said it all.

"Does he have a local address?" Hit with a sudden urgency, Lauren tapped the new accounts desk with a finger.

"I'm not sure I can give you that information," Carol said, glancing around the lobby.

"Please. I need to see him."

Carol studied her face. "Don't tell him I told you."

Lauren made a slashing motion across her mouth.

Carol stood and leaned into whisper in Lauren's ear. "Sixty Elm Street."

"Thanks. I owe you." Lauren hurried out the door and returned to the shop. She burst through the front door.

"Kennedy, I have to go." Without waiting for Kennedy's response, Lauren dashed to her car and plugged the address into her phone.

She arrived at the address on Elm Street and pulled into the driveway. Taking a deep breath, she climbed out of the car and strode to the front door.

The chime echoed inside but no one answered the door. She raised her hand and knocked. Then again.

"Where is he?" she said, looking up.

Her feet dragged as she headed back to her car. Disappointment weighed like a wet blanket on her shoulders.

"Well?" Kennedy asked the minute Lauren stepped through the bakery door.

"No. He wasn't there."

"Where was he? When will he be back?" Kennedy's questions hit her like hot grease splashing from a fry pan.

"I don't know.' Lauren sank onto a stool and dropped her head in her hands.

"You dropped this," Kennedy said, sliding the bank letter across the island. "Do you think he did this because of you?"

"I don't know what to think."

Kennedy's brow furrowed. "What's going on? I thought you liked him."

"I did. I do. Argghh. It's complicated."

"Spill it, girl." Kennedy dropped onto a stool across the counter.

"Remember when I told you about my ex? The guy from South Africa? Turns out he and Paul are brothers."

Kennedy gasped. "No way."

"My ex, Nigel, showed up at my house Monday and

so did Paul. Nigel made it sound like he and I slept together. Paul punched him in the face and then took off."

"Sounds like the creep deserved it."

"But now Paul thinks I slept with his brother. Or half-brother."

Kennedy examined her nails. "According to my romance novels, this is where the two main characters have a huge make-up session and clear the air. Then comes the happily-ever-after."

Lauren made a sound of disgust. "Yeah, right. Me, a small-town bakery owner struggling to survive and an uber-wealthy hot guy? I don't think so."

"It's one of the major romance tropes. Don't dis the trope."

Lauren scooted the stool back and stood. "Can you close up? I need to go lick my wounds."

"Trope," Kennedy said with a smile.

# Chapter 30

After the early-morning rush, Lauren returned to the kitchen to drown her sorrows in a batch of cupcakes for an upcoming wedding.

"Can you handle the front?"

Kennedy nodded. "You've got it."

The bell over the door jingled as another customer entered. "I'm on it," Kennedy said, striding to the front.

Lauren could hear Kennedy chatting with a man. She strained to hear the conversation and was disappointed it wasn't Paul's voice. Would it always be this way? Hoping for someone or something that would never work?

Brushing away the tears forming in the corners of her eyes, she focused on the recipe in front of her. A wedding might be the distraction needed. Who needed a man, anyway? After Nigel, she'd survived singlehood by thrusting her energy into the bakery.

Now that the shop wasn't in danger of having to close, she could carry on and perhaps expand.

*Who am I kidding?*

Expansion? Nope. Not without a huge influx of money.

Lauren's phone chimed with an incoming call from

Samantha.

"Hey, Sis. I wanted to give you a heads up. Mom is going to call you. Gird your loins, she's on a tear. She's threatening to fly up from Florida to see us since my shoot down there in the Sunshine State was cancelled."

"Thanks for the warning. How can we keep her away?"

"I'm thinking of feigning Covid."

"Ooh, good one. I'll have to come up with something too."

"Let me know, so I can corroborate your story."

"What's going on with your stalker?"

Sam's voice grew strained. "The police say they're following up on leads, but there doesn't seem to seem to be much progress. I'm thinking of taking some time off and hiding out somewhere."

"That sounds like a good idea."

"Yeah, but my agent wants me to finish out my contracts. She's worried I'll lose my momentum if I go on hiatus. I only have a couple of years until I'll be too old."

Lauren snorted. "Too old at twenty-five?"

"It is what it is. I could quit now and live comfortably for the next couple of years. After that …"

"You can always come work for me."

Sam laughed. "You know that would be a disaster. I only know how to make scrambled eggs."

"I love you, Sam," Lauren said.

"Love you too. Talk soon."

Conversations with Samantha always lifted Lauren's spirits. But as soon as they disconnected, Lauren's mood returned to depression.

Her head swung up when Kennedy strode into the

kitchen with a huge grin.

"You'll never believe it. That was Marvin, Paul's assistant. Guess what he did?"

"Who, Paul? Or Marvin?"

"Paul." Kennedy leaned a hip against the island. "They were staying in an Air B&B here in Hornell. Paul bought it and gave it to Marvin. Can you believe that?"

"And this concerns me, why?"

Kennedy rolled her eyes and held up a finger. "First, Paul is a good guy. Generous." Another finger. "Second, I found out where he lives in The City." Another finger. "Third, you need to talk to him. Marvin said he's pining." This was in air quotes.

Lauren stood and carried the cupcake tin to the oven. "I can hardly see him 'pining'."

"Oh, he's pining all right. Marvin said he's stress-eating like he's never seen."

Lauren closed the oven with a bang. "Right. Stress-eating over me."

"That's what Marvin said. And he knows the guy better than anyone."

"Whatever." Lauren grabbed a leftover muffin and picked off a piece, jamming it in her mouth.

"This is where you show up at his apartment in New York and you two fall into each other's arms."

Lauren raised her eyebrows and took another bite. "Trope?"

"Of course," Kennedy said with a smug smile.

"Not this time." Lauren stood and walked to the stairs leading up to her apartment. "I'm going to check on Molly."

Paul decided a change of scenery would do him good. Wandering around the house on Keuka Lake reminded him of Lauren. He imagined her stretched out on the sofa or standing on the deck overlooking the water. Even shopping for a boat didn't distract him from visions of her gliding over the lake, wind blowing her hair.

"Take me to The City," he instructed Marvin.

"Sure thing. When do you want to leave?"

"As soon as possible," Paul told him.

Marvin arranged for a helicopter to meet them at the Elmira Corning airport for the ride to New York City.

"Do you need me to go in with you?" Marvin asked over the rotor blades when they landed on Paul's rooftop.

"No. Thank you. I'll be in touch." Paul jumped out and crouched under the twirling blades until he was out of range.

His penthouse had been opened and refreshed by the staff. Paul shed his suit jacket and dropped it on the sofa. Loosening his tie, he strode to the window to look down on the street below. A glimpse of Central Park's green lawns gleamed in the distance. It always amazed him that a jewel like Central Park existed in the middle of concrete and steel. So American. Which is why he loved his adopted country.

In the massive bedroom, Paul shed his dress shirt and slacks and tossed them on the bed. He changed into a short-sleeved cotton shirt and loose-fitting jeans.

At least they'd been loose-fitting before he'd gone

on a junk food binge. Patting his stomach, Paul vowed to head to the building's gym. Tomorrow. Maybe.

The refrigerator yielded Paul's favorite healthy foods. Fruit, veggies, and lean cuts of meat. Before preparing a meal, he checked his phone for messages.

Nothing from Lauren. What did he expect? An apology? He was the one who should apologize. After Nigel admitted he and Lauren hadn't slept together, Paul should have reached out.

What are you afraid of, you twit?

The same thing every man is afraid of—rejection. He'd been a total cad to Lauren. How could he have believed Nigel's ugly accusation?

While he cooked, a plan began to form.

# Chapter 31

"**Lauren, I'm going** to be in New York tomorrow to see your sister."

Mom's voice pierced Lauren's ear.

"I thought Sam had Covid."

"I'm not worried. I've been vaccinated. I'll wear a mask."

Lauren chewed her lip, waiting for the other shoe to drop.

"You have to come to The City, so I can see both my girls." And there it was. Like a royal command.

"Mom, you know I can't just drop what I'm doing here at the bakery to run to New York."

"I happen to know you have a very capable employee. Besides, you can drive over Saturday after you close and go back late Monday evening."

Darn you, Sam.

"I don't know—"

"Oh, come on, sweetie. It'll be fun. I'll take you both shopping. I'm sure you can use some new clothes."

There it was again. The subtle hint Lauren wasn't good enough. Shopping with Mom meant trying on clothes in a size only a child could squeeze into. Or a runway model. Like Sam.

It was no use trying to refuse. Mom would continue to browbeat her into submission.

"Fine. I'll be there." Was it possible to lose fifty pounds before the weekend?

Lauren found Kennedy at the register helping a gaggle of silver-haired women wearing ridiculous red hats. A couple of the ladies stared in disdain at Kennedy's tattoo-covered arms.

"Need any help?" Lauren asked.

"Nope," Kennedy responded with a warm smile. "Just about done."

When the women had their muffins and moved toward the coffee station, Lauren pulled Kennedy aside. "I'm going to New York after we close Saturday. I got the royal summons."

Kennedy groaned. "Your mom?"

"Yup. It'll be fine. Sam can act as my bodyguard.

Kennedy's face took on a sly look. "I'll text you Paul's address."

"Oh, good grief, Ken. Let it go. We are not characters in one of your romance novels."

"Nevertheless, you might, oh, I don't know, need a ride somewhere. Or you might get stranded in Manhattan and need rescuing." Kennedy shrugged. "A girl can dream, right?"

"Dream on, sister. Now come help me frost those cupcakes."

Paul drummed his fingers on the arm of the sofa while waiting for a response from his attorney. Trying not to second-guess himself, he reviewed his plan to get Lauren to see him face-to-face, so he could apologize. And see if she felt the same as he did.

He couldn't live without her. Plain and simple, he had fallen for her. He wouldn't blame her if she hated his guts. He hated his own guts. Guilt over his parents' deaths still haunted him. Hours spent with a therapist helped somewhat, but the argument he'd had on the phone while his dad was driving still made him wonder.

Paul thought back to that day. He'd wanted to talk with Da about an idea he had for expanding in the US. The Bluetooth connection in Da's car kept cutting out, frustrating Paul and causing him to shout into the phone.

"We'll talk when we get to our hotel," Da had said.

"I need an answer now!"

It was after that the phone went dead. The car went off the road, over an embankment, and rolled over onto its bonnet. Mom had died instantly, but Da held on for two excruciating days. Paul sat by his bed, holding his dad's hand and begging him for forgiveness. His dad never regained consciousness.

Paul's quick temper had only increased after that. A Bible verse from long ago came to mind.

"So then, my beloved brethren, let every may be swift to hear, slow to wrath; for the wrath of man does not produce the righteousness of God."

Fat lot of good that was to him now. He'd exploded in anger at Nigel and blasted that anger toward Lauren.

His phone buzzed with a call from Ms. Kennolyn.

"Sir, I've sent the letter you requested via overnight mail. Is there anything else?"

"No, I think that's all. Thank you."

After disconnecting, Paul sent up a quick prayer, hoping God was still listening. "Make this work, please."

# Chapter 32

**"I'm heading out**," Lauren said to Kennedy after they'd closed the bakery. "Molly is ready and anxious for you. I actually think she likes you better than me."

"It's William. He's the puppy whisperer."

"I'm dreading the drive to The City. Parking is always a nightmare."

"But you never know who you might run into." Kennedy sent her a cheeky grin.

Lauren shook a finger in her direction. "Don't you go saying anything to Marvin."

Kennedy slashed a finger over her lips.

Slinging her purse over one shoulder, Lauren grabbed the handle of her rolling suitcase and headed out to her car. She knew the way to New York City by heart. On the drive, she connected her phone to listen to a book on Audible. Not a romance.

Kennedy was determined to make Lauren's life into a Hallmark movie. In real life, people didn't live happily ever after. Or at least it was rare. In real life people's feelings got hurt beyond repair. Misunderstandings happened.

She only half-listened to the crime drama pouring out of the car's speakers. The book was interrupted by an incoming call from Kennedy.

"Lauren, you got a certified letter from that New York attorney who's helping with your identity theft. I signed for it. Hope that's okay."

"Why are you still at the bakery?" Lauren asked.

"I'm just cleaning up the last of the mess in the dining room before I deliver those wedding cupcakes. Want me to open the letter?"

Lauren blew out a breath. "Sure."

Crackling noise came through the Bluetooth.

"It says, 'Dear Ms. Jensen, Would you be able to come to our offices Sunday, June 24 at 10:00 a.m. to sign the final paperwork for your identity theft case? We have successfully settled the case and would like to close the file. Please respond via email or phone at your earliest convenience.'"

"A meeting on a Sunday? I guess attorneys must work twenty-four seven."

"Want me to respond for you?"

"Sure. Thanks, Ken. Text me the address, okay?"

They disconnected and Lauren's phone chirped with Kennedy's text. At least this might get her out of spending the entire weekend with Mom. Small blessings.

By Saturday evening, Lauren was ready to do two things: drop onto Sam's couch and hide under a blanket and shoot her mom.

"That was fun," Sam commented when Lauren slipped her shoes off.

"Fun. Yeah."

"This calls for wine." While Samantha busied herself in the kitchen opening a bottle of wine, Lauren pulled her phone from her purse. She hadn't glanced at it all day. Mom had kept them busy going from store to store until Lauren wanted to scream. Thank God Mom had declined to stay at Samantha's place.

Lauren scrolled through a text from Kennedy with a photo of William cuddling Molly. She sent a heart emoji.

Then her heart stopped when there was a text from Paul.

**Paul**: Can we talk?

Paul gave up after obsessively checking every five minutes for a response from Lauren. He'd sent the text at noon, and it was now after seven.

Bugger. She must still be furious. Perhaps his plan for tomorrow would melt some of the ice he'd helped form around her heart.

Until then, it was time to make some amends. He composed a text to Nigel and backspaced to delete it. Trying again, he chose his words carefully.

**Paul**: Nigel, I'm sure our father had his reasons for doing what he did. Since he's gone, we will never know those reasons. It is up to us to honor his life. Can we do that? Together? I deeply regret cutting you out of my life. If you can forgive me, I'd like to start over. Let's get together over a meal the next time you're in New York.

He read it, reread it, and pressed send.

That done, Paul wandered around the penthouse and prayed for tomorrow's meeting.

# Chapter 33

"**Mom, I already** told you I have a meeting at ten. I'll catch up with you for lunch." Lauren practically shoved her mother out the door of Samantha's apartment. "Go with Sam, have fun, and I'll see you later."

"Promise?"

Lauren almost felt sorry for her. Almost. But after yesterday's battle over clothing choices …

"You don't want that," Mom had said when Lauren picked out a flowing dress in various shades of blue. "It looks like you're trying to hide your size."

Which was the desired result of her choice.

She and Sam had exchanged raised eyebrows and eye rolls. Sam tried to distract their mother, but once Mom was on a mission, she had the force of a tsunami. Lauren ended up with a nice pair of black slacks and a flowered top that covered arms to her elbows. "Don't want to show off those flabby arms," Mom had said.

If body-shaming was a sport, Mom was an Olympian.

"Come on, Mom," Sam said, guiding their mother out the door. Leaning in, she whispered to Lauren. "Let me know how it goes. If you don't want to meet us for lunch, I'll make an excuse."

"Thanks."

After enough time had passed and Lauren assumed they were on their way to the stores, Lauren descended the elevator and hailed a taxi. She arrived at the address she'd received from the letter and stared up at the building.

Montrose Tower.

Who did he think he was, Trump? Who has a building named after him?

Billionaires, that's who.

Lauren double-checked the floor number before stepping from the heat into the air-conditioned building. A uniformed guard sat behind a curved reception area.

"I'm here to see Ms. Kennolyn."

"Sign here, please," the guard said, shoving a clipboard across the wood surface. No other names appeared on the sheet. Lauren added her name and phone number and slid it back.

"Thank you, Ms. Jensen. Ms. Kennolyn is expecting you on the eleventh floor."

Lauren thanked him and walked to the elevators, her low-heeled sandals clicking on the marble floor. The lobby smelled of fresh lemons and clean laundry. She inhaled, savoring the scent, and exhaled to calm her nerves.

There was no reason to be nervous. Yes, this was Paul's building, but it wasn't his home address. According to Kennedy, he lived somewhere in Upper Manhattan.

The elevator rose in silence to the eleventh floor. The doors slid open to an impressive lobby. Dark wood furniture and hunter green carpet invited her to step in to luxury. Her feet sank into the plush pile.

Before she took a few steps, an older woman poked her head out of an office.

"There you are," she exclaimed with a smile. "I thought I heard the elevator."

"I'm Susan Kennolyn." She approached with her hand out to shake Lauren's.

"I'm glad you could make it on such short notice. We'll be meeting in the conference room. Did you have any trouble finding us?" The woman's chatter immediately calmed Lauren's nervousness.

She was ushered into a large room with the longest wooden table Lauren had ever seen. She counted fifteen chairs circling around its shiny maple finish.

Susan ushered her to a seat on one side. "I'll be right back with those papers. Please make yourself comfortable. There's coffee and water on the credenza. Help yourself."

Instead of sitting, Lauren wandered to the window to take in the view. Between two of the skyscrapers, she caught a glimpse of Central Park. Maybe she and Sam could talk Mom into a carriage ride through the park. Anything to distract her from more shopping.

The door to the conference room opened. Lauren swung around and gasped.

"I was hoping you'd show up," Paul said, watching Lauren for any hint she might bolt from the room.

"You tricked me."

Paul took a step closer. "I had to. You didn't answer my text."

Lauren crossed her arms over her chest. "What did you expect? You thought Nigel and I …"

"I was wrong."

The words hung in the air between them.

"I'm the worse kind of idiot," Paul continued. "Nigel told me everything. He said you refused to even kiss him. 'A kiss is a promise' you'd said."

Lauren's slow nod encouraged him to continue.

"I judged you unfairly and I'm sorry. There's so much you don't know about Nigel, our father, the accident—"

"I want to know."

Paul's heart swelled. She hadn't run, hadn't moved. He stepped around the end of the conference table to join her at the window. "I want to tell you everything. I want you to know who I am. Why I gained so much weight. And lost it. Why I fly off the handle."

Lauren's palm was warm against his cheek. He closed his eyes and pressed against her hand.

Her voice was soft when she spoke. "A kiss is a promise."

Paul's eyes flew open. Lauren's face was inches from his. "A promise," he said, and lowered his lips to hers.

Hours later, Lauren looked at her phone and gasped. "I totally forgot I was supposed to meet my mom and sister for lunch. Mom is going to kill me." And make me ashamed to be me.

She composed a quick text to Samantha.

**Lauren**: Sorry.

"I want to meet this amazing woman who gave birth to you," Paul said.

"No, you don't. She'll eat you for dinner."

Paul smiled. "I've faced wolves around the conference table trying to take over my business. I've outbid sharks on projects. I think I can handle your mom."

Lauren planted a kiss on his cheek. "Don't say I didn't warn you."

She placed a quick call to Samantha. "Sam, I'm so sorry. Things got a little complicated here at the attorney's office. Can we meet for dinner?"

Paul gestured to himself. "My treat," he mouthed. He pointed his phone screen toward her. Paul had dropped a pin at Le Bernardin.

Lauren nodded. "I'm sending you the location now."

"Looks expensive," Samantha said. "Let me check with Mom. I'm not sure she has the budget for that."

Lauren sent Paul a smile. "Someone else is paying."

Sam's silence said it all. Finally, she said, "Well, okay then. See you there. What time?"

"Six?" She sent a questioning look at Paul, and he nodded.

"Anything you want to tell me?" Sam asked.

"Nope." Lauren disconnected and laughed.

"I love to hear you laugh," Paul said, gathering her in is arms.

Lauren leaned against his chest and listened to his heartbeat against her cheek. She could stay here. The words whispered in her spirit. Stay here, in this man's arms. Forever.

Paul pulled away and regarded her with warm eyes.

"Let's get you back to your sister's to change."

Lauren mentally shook herself, mood broken. "Of course."

Time to put on the armor she'd need to deflect Mom's barbs.

# Chapter 34

"I hope this is suitable for that fancy restaurant," Lauren said, turning this way and that while Paul waited on Samantha's comfy sofa.

He rose and approached her. "You look wonderful."

She'd twisted her hair into a loose French twist and applied mascara to her pale lashes. A bit of color on her lips and she felt as ready as possible.

"I like that outfit." Paul grasped her shoulders and placed a kiss on her cheek. "I won't mess up your lipstick."

Disappointed but charmed, Lauren smiled. "Thanks."

Paul released his hold, and she reached for a sweater she'd found in her sister's closet. Remarkably, it fit, though a tad snug.

"Well, as my sister would say when meeting our mom, gird up your loins."

Paul threw back his head and laughed. Lauren joined him, delighted in the dimple making an appearance low on his cheek. His laugh wasn't the braying laugh of someone forcing themselves to be in agreement. Rather it was true and strong, and Lauren felt a deep sense of satisfaction she could make this man laugh.

"Let's go then," Paul said, crooking his elbow for her hand. He wore his usual suit and Lauren thought he was the handsomest man in the world. She was lucky to have him.

They arrived at the restaurant and were immediately escorted to a booth in a private corner.

"You've been here before?" Lauren asked.

"It's one of my favorites when I'm in the City."

She scooted over to make room for him and spied her mother and Samantha following the Matre'd to their table.

"Hello again," Paul said to Samantha, taking her hand. Lauren noticed the calculating look on Mom's face as Paul planted a kiss on Samatha's cheek. "And you must be Mrs. Jensen." He shook Mom's hand.

"Please call me Margo."

They slid into the booth, Samantha next to Lauren and Mom on the end across from Paul. Mom seemed disappointed, though Lauren couldn't think why.

"Samantha tells me you recently purchased a house on Keuka Lake," Mom said.

"That is correct. I'm pleased with the remodel and plan to extend the improvements to the basement. I've decided to make the house my main residence."

"Oh? Why is that?"

"Living in the City exhausts me. All the noise, the traffic, constant movement. I prefer the quiet of the country. It reminds me of England."

Before her mom could respond, a waiter appeared with a silver bucket full of ice and a bottle protruding from it. He was immediately followed by another waiter bearing four champagne glasses on a tray.

"Ah, thank you." They watched and the bottle was uncorked, and four glasses of bubbly wine were poured.

"What's the occasion?" Mom asked as Paul raised his glass in a toast.

Paul smiled and Lauren appreciated the dimple making another appearance. "It isn't every day I get to have dinner with three beautiful women." He leaned forward to lightly clink his glass to theirs.

Lauren took a sip of the wine, wrinkling her nose as it tickled.

"I took the liberty of ordering," Paul said. "I hope that's all right."

Lauren glanced to Sam and their mother.

"So wonderful to have a man take charge," Mom said.

Lauren narrowed her eyes when Mom's agreement seemed a little over the top.

The pressure from Paul's thigh against hers was enough to calm her frazzled nerves. A meal with Mom was usually full of barely veiled comments about Lauren's food choices.

Mom set her glass down and smiled. "Did you know Samantha is a runway model?"

"I believe Lauren mentioned that, yes," Paul replied.

"She's not only beautiful, but talented as well. My only disappointment is she chose not to go to college. But then, with her looks, college was not her first choice."

Lauren squirmed under her mother's unspoken comparison.

When Paul didn't respond, Mom continued. "Samantha has always been such a delight."

Lauren bit the inside of her lip. Was Mom really trying to throw her sister at Paul?

Paul raised his glass again. "I'm sure you're proud of both of your girls, Margo."

"Of course." Mom seemed reluctant to concede whatever point she was attempting to make.

He turned slightly to face Lauren. "I'm sure you are aware Lauren's bakery is a huge success in Hornell. I'm amazed she started the business all on her own and has managed to make it what it is—a place for the community to gather."

Lauren shot him a grateful look.

"She created the idea for a mug wall." He went on to describe in great detail the pegboard, the assortment of mugs, and the labels for the regular customers.

There was a flurry of movement across the restaurant as a group of suit-wearing men entered. A tall man in the middle seemed to be escorted by the others.

The man came to a stop by their table.

"Paul Montrose," he said, reaching out to shake Paul's hand. Paul made a motion to stand, but the man stopped him. "No, don't get up. Looks like you're enjoying yourself. Three women, Paul?" He laughed. "By the way, thank you for your generous contribution to my campaign." With a flick of his hand, he and his entourage continued toward the back of the room.

Lauren forced her mouth to move. "Was that . . ."

Paul grinned. "The presidential candidate? Yes."

Mom still gaped. "You know him?" Mom managed to force out.

"I don't *know* know him. We've crossed paths a few times." Paul shrugged as if it was of no significance.

Lauren eyes were wide when she turned her attention back to him. She was so out of her league.

Paul was embarrassed by the little exchange with the current presidential nominee. He meant his donations to be private, not something to be celebrated.

Unlike this get-together. He wasn't fooled for a moment Lauren's mother meant for his attention to be drawn to Lauren's sister. Yes, she was beautiful. But so thin Paul had to wonder if she was anorexic. It wouldn't surprise him. With a mother like theirs, no wonder Lauren turned to baking and sampling her wares for comfort. It appeared Samantha starved herself in order to insulate herself from their mother's constant attention to appearance.

Pressing his thigh more firmly against Lauren's, he nodded toward the approaching waiter. "Ah, here comes our first course."

No one spoke as the waiter set plates of a warm artichoke salad. He watched as Sam daintily picked at her food, while Lauren dove in. He appreciated her enjoyment of a fine meal, grateful she had an appetite that rivaled his.

While they ate, he imagined them working in the kitchen of the lake house, side by side, creating delicious and healthy food.

His musing was interrupted by Margo. "Lauren, you shouldn't eat so fast. It might upset your stomach."

Paul's jaw tightened as fury rose fast and hot to warm his face. Before Lauren could respond, he placed a hand over hers.

"I'm sure she's fine, Margo." He sent Lauren what he hoped was an encouraging smile. "Besides, I love a woman with a hearty appetite."

Margo's lips tightened. He saw the ghost of a smile touch Samantha's lips. Score one for him.

Not to be outdone, Margo set her fork down and took a sip of her bubbly. "Lauren has always struggled with her weight. I blame it on allowing her to shovel her food down too quickly."

*Game on, mum.* Paul leaned back and stretched an arm over the back of the booth, allowing his hand to caress Lauren's shoulder. "I find a woman with curves much more attractive than some waif who looks like she could blow away in a gust of wind."

When Margo glanced down at her plate, Paul winked at Lauren's sister. She covered her mouth with a napkin, hiding the smile he knew lurked there.

When their plates were cleared and the maln course served, Paul said, "I believe this salmon is caught in the Thousand Islands area. I'm purchasing a house there."

Lauren's mother watched him, her gaze unreadable. "But of course, I'll need someone to help me decorate it, won't I, love?" He leaned toward Lauren and planted a kiss on her cheek. That should send a signal even Margo couldn't miss. Rather like driving a lorry through the front of a China shop.

He noted with amusement Margo's face diffuse with color.

"Lauren is great with color-coordinating and such," Samantha chimed in. "You haven't been to her apartment. Yet." She emphasized the word yet with the business end of her fork. "But you'll see how cute it's decorated."

Paul sent a questioning look in Lauren's direction. She hadn't said a word in several minutes, seeming content to enjoy the delicious fish and leek-truffle Marinière

He waited for Margo to reload her weapon. He didn't have to wait long.

"Paul, you have an interesting accent. Where are you from?"

"I'm originally from Durbin, South Africa. I moved to the UK with my parents after what you call middle school."

Margo seemed to be thinking. "Durbin? Lauren, didn't you have a boyfriend from there?"

Lauren choked and covered her mouth with her napkin.

"Here, love, have a sip of water." Paul lifted the water glass and waited for Lauren to take it.

He looked Margo square in the face. "Yes, Margo. Lauren's former boyfriend, Nigel is also from Durbin. He's my half-brother."

Now Margo choked. She'd hoped to score a point, but Paul had beaten her to it.

"Let's not ruin this lovely meal by dwelling on the past, shall we? I can't wait for dessert."

He pulled his arm from around Lauren's shoulder and ate several bites of his fish. "I'm so glad Lauren doesn't get airsick. She did great on our little jaunt to the Gabreski Airport, didn't you?"

Paul waited while another waiter arrived with a bottle of white wine and four glasses. Paul sampled the wine and nodded his approval. When the wine was poured and conversation lulled, Paul continued to throw barbs in Lauren's mum's direction.

"What do you think, Lauren, does this restaurant rate over an eight point five? I remember you rating our lunch at Fauna after our limo ride."

"No, I rated our date there at eight point five. The restaurant was a definite nine."

Good, she was back to herself. Turning to face her, he said, "And here?"

She took a sip of the wine, held it in her mouth, and swallowed. "Nine point nine." That she smiled into his eyes wasn't missed by her mum.

"You had a lunch date at Fauna?"

Paul laid a hand over Lauren's on the table. "Our first."

Samantha snickered. "Get a room, you two. This is getting embarrassing."

"Samantha," Margo said with a scowl. "Don't be vulgar."

"Relax, Mom. Lauren knows I'm kidding."

Paul leaned over and whispered in Lauren's ear. "The first of many dates."

He watched as a slow blush crept from her neck to her cheeks.

By the time they'd had dessert and coffee, Paul was ready to drop. Though he hadn't exactly thawed Margo to room temperature, she was at least not still trying to fling him in Samantha's direction.

When they stepped outside to hail a taxi, Paul didn't bother to hide his intentions by pulling Lauren in for a long and lingering kiss. Her mother's gasp satisfied him more than any business deal.

"I'd love to take you ladies for breakfast tomorrow," he said as they climbed into a waiting taxi.

Paul wasn't disappointed when Margo declined.

"I have an early flight back to Florida. Thank you anyway."

Paul assisted Margo into the cab and waited while she scooted over to make room for Samantha. Before Lauren could reach for the passenger door, Paul pulled her back.

"Stay for a bit. I'll get you to your sister's place later."

Lauren glanced at the waiting cab and back at him. "Okay."

# Chapter 35

**Lauren watched her** mother's face as the cab pulled away from the curb. Her mouth was open, and she seemed to be speaking to the driver who ignored her. Sam gave her a wave and a smile as the cab merged into the traffic.

"Well, that was fun," she said, turning to Paul.

He sent her a grim smile. "You did warn me."

The taxi he'd hailed pulled to the curb. "Can I take you to my apartment?"

Lauren narrowed her eyes. "As long as you don't compromise my morals, Mr. Montrose."

"Never that. I'd have to answer to your mum."

Twin emotions swelled in Lauren's chest—freedom and security. Mom's head had looked ready to explode when Paul finally made it clear she was the one he wanted. Not Samatha. She felt a little sorry for her mother. But only a little. The flaming darts she'd lobbed in Lauren's direction still burned.

Paul placed a hand over hers on the seat between them. "Let's never let misunderstandings come between us again. Every moment I was away from you felt like punishment."

Lauren found it difficult to grab a breath. "I know."

"When we get to my apartment, let's talk. I'll tell you about my parents, Nigel, and anything else you want to know."

The taxi pulled to a stop outside a tall building with a covered entrance. A uniformed guard stood outside the door underneath the bright red canopy. He glanced right and left as they climbed out of the car and opened the door using a card to swipe the keypad.

"Welcome back, Mr. Montrose."

"Thank you, Jamison. I'll text you when my guest is ready to leave. Perhaps at that time you can call a cab for her?"

"Of course. No Marvin this evening?"

"He is staying in Hornell for a few days."

"Very good, sir."

Lauren kept silent during the exchange. Suddenly insecure, she clutched Paul's arm. "Are you sure . . ."

"I'm sure I want to spend some uninterrupted time with you." His eyes pooled with concern. "Are you all right? We can go someplace public if that makes you feel better."

Lauren studied his face. "No, I'm okay."

Paul used a fob to activate the elevator. It rose to the top floor whisper quiet. The doors opened up to an enormous living room. His penthouse decried the description he'd given her of his 'apartment.'

"This place is big enough for three of mine to fit," Lauren said, wandering from the fireplace to the cozy seating arrangement around an imported rug. She touched the back of the dark leather sofa, marveling at its softness. The room exuded warmth, though the sky outside was lit only by an eyelash of a moon. An open paperback book lay on the coffee table. Lauren bent over to inspect the book, smiling when she saw the title. *The Lincoln Lawyer*.

"Do you like my apartment?" Paul seemed eager for her approval.

"I do. But I think I prefer the house on Keuka Lake."

Paul joined her at the window. Their breath formed tiny circles of condensation.

"I prefer it as well." He inhaled and exhaled with a whoosh. "Could you see yourself living there?"

"What are you saying?" Lauren's stomach felt like she'd swallowed a beehive. They'd known each other for, what a couple of weeks? Been on one date and then the disaster of the lunch at his house. Was it possible to fall in love so quickly?

Paul's hand was warm as he grasped hers. "I'm saying I want to have a future with you. I hope you feel the same."

"Are you sure you want me now that you've met my mother?"

One corner of his mouth rose. "I can handle your mum. She'll warm up once she gets a taste of what I can offer her daughter."

Lauren's eyebrows rose. "Oh really? What can you offer her daughter? I mean, it's all well and good to have your own jet and a house on an island."

Paul took her shoulders and turned her to face him. "I can offer you my heart. I can assure you it's worth more than a billion dollars."

"Is that so?" Lauren smiled. "I guess that would be okay." She leaned forward to kiss him.

Before their lips met, Paul said, "And in case I forgot to tell you, you are beautiful. And I plan to tell you that every single day."

In that moment, she believed him. Paul didn't care if she carried extra pounds. He saw beyond her size and into her heart.

TWO MONTHS LATER

"You're doing what?" Kennedy's exclamation burst from her lips.

"I'm giving you the Muffin Top."

They stood in the kitchen after the shop closed on Saturday afternoon.

"If you're kidding, I'm going to toss you in the oven, Lauren."

Lauren shook her head. "Not kidding. It's all arranged. You only have to sign the papers. The loan is paid off and the building, including the apartment, is yours. If you want it."

"Want it?" Kennedy seemed incapable of saying anything except repeating Lauren's words.

"If you don't want it—"

"Don't want it? Now you *are* kidding."

Lauren drew Kennedy in for a hug. "It's yours. You can run it, sell it, or burn it to the ground. Once you sign the deed, it's yours."

"I can't believe it. Nothing like this happens to me."

"Believe it. Paul and I discussed it, and it makes the most sense. I'm going to be busy with wedding preparations and helping decorate the Thousand Islands house."

Kennedy sank onto a stool as if her legs couldn't

hold her. "I can't believe it," she whispered.

Lauren looked around the kitchen, knowing she'd miss this place. Wandering into the dining room, she let her hand run across the glass display case. The mug wall had been such a success it had brought in more customers, even some coming from as far as Dansville and Canaseraga.

The coffee thermoses had been dismantled and sat upside down on a towel to dry. Every table gleamed spotless. Kennedy would do a great job running the business. Especially without the financial burden of having to make a monthly loan payment. Even William had started working a few hours after school, washing mixing bowls and clearing debris.

She returned to the kitchen to find Kennedy wiping tears from her cheeks with a paper towel.

"And I forgot to tell you. Certified Canine Services felt that Molly was a bit too rambunctious for a support dog. They're bringing her back here tomorrow. I'd like you to have her."

"For real?"

"For real. William needs a dog. Besides, Paul isn't a fan of that sweet mutt."

Kennedy's grin practically split her face in half. She bent over her phone and started tapping.

"Who are you texting? William?"

Kennedy glanced up with a guilty look. "No. Marvin."

Lauren burst into laughter. "Okay. Let me know how that progresses. I'm heading to Paul's to work on wedding stuff."

Kennedy barely spared her a glance as Lauren gathered her purse and headed out the door.

"Well, that's about it," Paul said, leaning back in one of the plush recliners. "Let's take a break."

Lauren tossed the pad of paper and pen she'd been using onto the coffee table and released a breath. "Let's walk to the end of the pier. I could use some fresh air."

"Brilliant idea." He stood and placed his hands on his hips, twisting at the waist. His back gave a satisfying crack. "Grab a sweater. The wind looks like it's kicked up."

Lauren returned from one of the bedrooms carrying a sweater. Paul couldn't get enough of watching her even doing something as mundane as pulling on a light wrap.

"What?" she asked, eyeing him.

"Nothing. I was thinking I'm the luckiest man in the world."

"Yes, you are," she agreed with a smile.

"Come on, let's get that fresh air you're craving and talk about something other than weddings."

They stepped outside and down the wooden steps to the whitewashed dock. Warmth from the summer sun radiated off the wood, contrasting with the breeze blowing across the surface of the lake.

"I never get tired of this," Lauren said, focusing her eyes on the distant sailboats bobbing on the water.

"Neither do I." But he wasn't looking at the lake, the water, or the boats.

"What do you want to talk about?" Lauren said as they sauntered hand in hand to the end of the dock.

"Do you want children?" Paul hadn't meant to blurt

it out like that, but the words hung between them.

"What brought this on?" Lauren asked, her face clouded with concern.

Paul sighed. "Since I've made peace with Nigel, I've realized how important it is for children to, oh, I don't know." He scrubbed a hand across his face. "I'm botching this up."

Lauren tugged his hand. "Yes, I want children. A dozen of them, if that's what you want."

Paul's chest swelled with love for this woman. "Well, at least two."

"When shall we get started on that?"

Paul pulled her in for a kiss. "The minute you say 'I do.'"

"That might be a little awkward. Can we at least wait until we get to the hotel after wedding?"

Paul pretended outrage. "If you insist."

"I do." Lauren started to laugh and shoved his chest. "Don't get any ideas mister. That was a practice 'I do.'"

"Of course." Paul gave a mock bow before pulling her in for a proper kiss.

THE END

Read on for the next in the Hearts of New York series – Billionaire and the Beauty – Available June 2025

Chapter 1

Samantha held the letter in a hand with shaking hands. How had he gotten so close without anyone seeing him? The stuffed brown teddy bear stared at her with black-button eyes.

*A gift for my best girl.*

The writing was scrawled, as if scratched onto the blank sheet in a hurry. It was signed,

*Love,*

*Your soon to be not so secret admirer*

Sam dropped the letter like it burned her fingers. It fluttered to the floor of her dressing room and lay face-up. Menacing. Dangerous.

Her phone chirped with a text. Her agent, Skyler.

**Skyler**: Almost ready for you.

Sam stared at her pale face reflected in the mirror. No way could she go out to the studio as if nothing had happened. She composed a text to Skyler.

**Sam**: I don't feel well. I have to cancel.

No one had ever accused Samantha Jensen of being a diva. But today, she'd open herself up to all kinds of criticism.

Instead of a response from Skyler, her agent burst through the dressing room door with a scowl.

"What's going on, Sam? We need you on the set, like, ten minutes ago."

Samantha leaned out of the canvas chair and plucked the letter from the floor with two fingers.

"Look." She thrust the letter in Skyler's direction.

Skyler's eyes widened and her mouth fell open. "How did he find you?" she whispered.

"I thought you said the police were closing in on him." Sam couldn't help her accusatory tone.

Skyler sank onto the uncomfortable sofa with a groan. "That's what they told me. They said they had a line on this crazy stalker." She raised tortured eyes to meet Sam's. "I'm so sorry."

"What am I going to do?" After weeks of rearranging Samantha's modeling contracts to throw off the stalker, things had been quiet on that front. At last feeling safe, Samantha had fulfilled some of the commitments Skyler had scheduled months ago.

Skyler got to her feet and dropped the letter onto the seat she vacated. "I'll take care of things out there." She flipped a hand toward the door. This was the Skyler Sam was used to. All business. "I'll make up an excuse. How would you like to come down with Covid? I'll let Dior know you won't be at the runway shoot next week."

"You'll take care of all the details?"

"I'm on it. You need to find a place to hide out. Change your appearance. Go off grid."

Sam let her head drop into her hands. Skyler made it sound simple.

***

Samantha hadn't left the rental house on Lake Skaneateles for three days. Each time she approached the French doors leading out to the massive wood deck, panic fluttered in her chest. What if her stalker found out where she was?

As impossible as that seemed, terror still haunted her sleep and held her captive during the day. The summer storm gave her a handy excuse to not venture out. But today, the sun had burned off the mist hovering over the lake and the soft breeze through the windows beckoned her outside.

With one last glance in the oval mirror over the dressing table, Samantha shoved her bare feet into a pair of flip flops and walked out to the living room. Her sister, Lauren had helped dye her blonde locks a dull shade of brown. Sam used a pair of kitchen shears to cut her hair to chin length. The bangs were uneven and hung over her eyebrows. Lauren had picked up the ugliest clothes she could find from the Goodwill store in Hornell before dropping Sam off at the rental.

"You look like a different person," Lauren had told her.

"That's the plan." They'd hugged goodbye, and Lauren had driven off to her fiancé's house on Keuka Lake.

Sam snagged the glass of iced tea she'd left sweating on the dining room table and stepped through the French doors onto the deck. Humidity rose like a sauna from the damp wood. Inhaling, she walked to the railing and looked out over the lake, blue and clear as an aquamarine.

"Why do I have to wear a life jacket?"

The girl's voice from the house next door pulled Sam's attention from the lake. From the vantage point of the deck, she could see down to the house next door.

A deck, the twin to her rental, led from the lower floor out onto the lake. A girl and a man stood facing each other, apparently arguing.

The man's voice stayed low and modulated, while the girl's rose in outrage.

"Because the water is cold and when you fall, I want you to be safe."

"When I fall? You mean if."

"Mandy, I'm not going to stand here and argue with you. Either wear the life jacket or go back in the house."

"You're so mean!"

Sam smiled as the girl stomped her foot. She judged her age at fourteen or fifteen. The drama ended when the girl snatched the life jacket from the deck and shoved her arms through it.

The man, presumably her dad, must have felt Sam's stare. He looked up, shading his eyes with one hand. Sam felt a flush work its way up from neck to forehead. She swiveled in the opposite direction. A few moments later, she heard the splash as the girl pushed off the deck on a paddle board.

Sam sighed. That looked fun. What would it have been like to enjoy the simple pleasure of learning to paddle board instead of posing for photos? Her childhood had been anything but normal. When Sam shot up to six feet at fourteen, Mom had dragged her to a modeling agency where she'd learned to flirt with the camera instead of boys.

Turning back, she watched the dad watch his daughter as she struggled to stand on the board and propel herself forward with the long paddle. She wobbled, got her balance, then tipped sideways into the lake.

The dad must have heard Sam's laugh. He tilted his face up to where she stood, shading his eyes again. She felt a flash of alarm and scurried back into the house. Skyler's voice echoed in her ears.

"Don't attract attention."

***

Logan Walters refused to argue with his fourteen-year-old daughter. Her mother may get worn down by Mandy's whining, but Logan was made of sterner stuff. Now that Mandy was living with him full-time, he needed to establish some firm boundaries. In the past, he'd indulged her every whim, hoping to make the most of their short times together.

Two weeks in the summer, a week in the winter, and an occasional weekend when Vivian wanted a break. Now that Vivian had flitted off to Italy with her new husband, he was Dad and Mom to his recalcitrant teen. He'd have to try hard to make up for his daughter being abandoned by his ex.

A movement from next door caught his eye. They had a new neighbor in the rental. He squinted up through the blinding sun reflecting off Lake Skaneateles to see. Definitely female, though it was difficult to tell with her baggy clothing. She better not be a partier like the last group. That had been a colossal mistake, renting to a group of college guys.

Logan turned his attention back to his daughter. She sulked while putting on the life jacket and continued to sulk until she turned her back on him and pushed the paddle board onto the water.

Mandy fell with a huge splash and Logan heard laughter from the upper deck next door. Shading his eyes again, he caught the woman covering her mouth as she laughed. As soon as she saw him looking, her smile disappeared, and she dashed into the house.

"Are you okay?" Logan called to Mandy.

Water dripped from his daughter's head and down her face. She held the board with one hand and used the other to sweep hair from her face.

"Fine," she sputtered.

Logan hid his grin. "I'm going inside to grab my laptop."

Mandy hauled herself back onto the board. "No pictures, Dad."

"I promise."

Logan returned a couple minutes later and set his laptop on the glass patio table. He'd be able to get some work done and watch Mandy at the same time. But first, find out who rented his house next door.